Suddenly, the library basement lights went out.

Frozen in blackness, Grace called out, "Hello, I'm down here."

A muffled shuffling sent terror pulsing through her veins. She slid along the cabinets, the handles jabbing her side. A rhythmic creaking filled her ears, the sound made louder in the blackness.

"I know you're down here," someone whispered.

Tiny pinpricks of fear blanketed Grace's scalp. She moved closer to the desk, realizing whoever it was had intentionally turned off the lights. Was coming for her.

Her hand found her tote bag on the desk. She reached inside for her phone. She swallowed hard. *Remain calm. You've been in far scarier situations.* Her usual response to those who warned her that her investigation was going to get her into trouble didn't seem to be doing her much good at this exact moment.

A groan of something heavy being moved cut through the blackness. Grace scrambled under the desk with her phone. A violent whoosh of air sent her hair flying away from her face, and a loud crash exploded in her ears...

Alison Stone lives with her husband of more than twenty years and their four children in Western New York. Besides writing, Alison keeps busy volunteering at her children's schools, driving her girls to dance and watching her boys race motocross. Alison loves to hear from her readers at Alison@AlisonStone.com. For more information, please visit her website, alisonstone.com. She's also chatty on Twitter, @alison_stone. Find her on Facebook at Facebook.com/alisonstoneauthor.

Books by Alison Stone

Love Inspired Suspense

PLAIN JEOPARDY

ALISON STONE

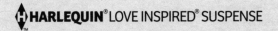

Recycling programs
for this product may
not exist in your area.

 LOVE INSPIRED BOOKS

ISBN-13: 978-1-335-54357-8

Plain Jeopardy

www.Harlequin.com

Printed in U.S.A.

Peace I leave with you, my peace I give unto you:
not as the world giveth, give I unto you.
Let not your heart be troubled, neither let it be afraid.
–John 14:27

To my eldest daughter, Kelsey,
as you get ready for your next adventure. I'm very proud
of you. May all your dreams come true. Love and kisses.

To Scott and the rest of the gang,
love you guys, always and forever.

ONE

The traction-control light lit up on the dashboard, and Grace Miller clutched the steering wheel tighter. The tires quickly gained purchase on the snowy country road. *Phew.* Not as icy as she'd feared. All she needed to do was leave a little extra distance between her car and the car in front of hers, which wasn't too hard to do on the deserted streets of Quail Hollow, New York. Not a lot of cars—or wagons—out after dark. Most people were hunkered down at home doing sane things like watching TV or reading a book, not chasing leads on a story on a snowy night in the Amish community.

Grace reached across and touched the crumpled handwritten note she had tossed onto the passenger seat.

I have info about drinking party. Meet at gas station. Main and Lapp. 8 p.m. Get gas while your there.

She could forgive the writer's misuse of the word *your* if it meant she had a new lead on a story that had, so far, produced nothing more than what had already been published in regional papers or played on the local TV stations out of Buffalo.

Grace had been surprised to find the handwritten note taped to the front door of her sister's bed & breakfast. She wondered why they hadn't knocked. She had been home alone most of the day, except for the window of time when Eli Stoltz, her sister's Amish neighbor, stopped by to care for the horses.

That would have been too easy. Instead, the author of the note had insisted on a clandestine meeting at a random location on a freezing night. Making her get out in the cold and pump gas, no less.

Already she didn't like the person. They better not waste her time.

Since she had zero leads, she didn't have much of a choice. The bishop had turned her away, and the sheriff's department had only given her the most basic of information regarding the party and the fatal accident that night. Even the few teenagers she'd tracked down had shut her out. However, Grace was not easily deterred. She had spent her days since graduating with her journalism degree traveling the world, writing in-depth articles featuring people or events that needed highlighting. The tagline under her online bio read Giving a Voice to the Voiceless.

Grace turned her car onto Main Street and was mildly cheered by the trees covered in twinkling white lights, even though Christmas had passed a few weeks ago. She supposed no one could fault the residents of Quail Hollow for looking for something to brighten up the long months of January and February in the great white north, where the days were short and the snow was deep.

It had been a long time since she had spent a winter up north. Her job afforded her the luxury of traveling the world, and when she had a choice, she chose warm, mild weather, certainly not polar-bear cold.

Before Grace's emergency appendectomy, she had finished a story in Florida about a young mother who had lost her job after she missed work due to cancer treatments. Grace's story led to a huge community outpouring of support and the promise of another job when the woman felt well enough.

That was why Grace did what she did.

But life's twists and turns—including a surprise appendectomy, infection and prolonged recovery—put her right in the middle of an exciting story while holed up at her sister's bed & breakfast in Quail Hollow.

Grace slowed and turned into the snowy parking lot of the gas station. The back of her car fishtailed, then she regained control. Prickles of anxiety swept across her skin. Boy, she hated driving in the snow. It didn't help that her sister's car probably needed new tires.

Grace pulled under the overhang meant to protect customers from the elements while they filled their tanks. The snow swirled violently, touching down in mini tornadoes. No overhang would protect the customers from those gusts. She shuddered, despite the warm air pumping from the heating vents. In the rearview mirror, she saw an Amish man with his collar flipped up, hunkered down in his wagon. He flicked the horse's reins and continued to trot down the street in a steady rhythm.

Suck it up, buttercup, she thought. At least *she* wasn't exposed to the elements like the Amish man in his open wagon. How did they deal with the harsh winter? It reminded her of a story she had written about the homeless in Arizona. One man claimed he moved down there from Minnesota because if life had dealt him the unfair hand of being homeless, he would choose to live in the desert.

Clearing her thoughts, Grace scanned the gas station parking lot. She had to keep her head in the game. Stay focused. The gas station and surrounding stores were mostly quiet except for a couple of vehicles parked along the fence on one edge of the parking lot. One car, covered in a layer of snow, was probably an employee's. The other, a truck, looked like someone had recently parked and run into the attached minimart or a neighboring store on Main Street.

No sign of someone lingering around to talk to her.

Clicking her fingernails on the steering wheel, she watched the red digital number on the dashboard change to 8:01 p.m. Past experience told her that sources didn't always keep to a schedule. Dreading the inevitable, she wrapped her scarf around her neck and pushed open the door. The arctic air rushed in, making her wish she was covering a story near the equator. "Where are you?" she muttered under her breath as she climbed out and scanned the parking lot again. It didn't help that she had no idea who she was looking for.

Grace waited half a second before lifting the pump from its slot and jamming it into the car's tank, hoping that the letter writer approached before her ears froze off. She yanked down her hat. Sighing heavily, she swiped her credit card through the reader, selected 87 octane and began pumping. Because she refused to ruin her nice leather gloves, she didn't wear them while she filled the tank. Seconds seemed like hours, and she wondered if she'd ever be able to uncurl her frozen fingers from the metal handle.

She continued to sweep her gaze across the area while she pumped gas. The pump clicked off. If her secret informant was going to show, he'd better show now or she was getting back into her car and cranking up the heat before she turned into a popsicle.

She turned to hang up the pump when she heard the deep rumble of an engine roaring to life. She spun around. The reverse lights lit up on the pickup truck parked nearby. Strange, since she hadn't noticed anyone getting into it. She reached for the door handle on her car, convinced her pen pal had stiffed her.

The sound of tires spinning drew her attention back to the truck. Her heart jolted into her throat. The driver sped in Reverse, barreling directly toward her.

She dove to the side, fearing she'd be pinned between her car and the gas pumps. Visions of news coverage of fuel pumps ablaze and charred cars ran through her mind. She landed with an *oomph* and pain shot through her midsection from her recent appendectomy. Slushy wetness seeped through her clothes, adding insult to injury.

The sound of metal crunching metal filled her ears. She desperately tried to scramble away in an awkward crab crawl. Craning her head, she caught sight of the pickup truck tearing out onto Main Street. Relief that he was leaving wrestled with anger that he was getting away, making her forget the pain shooting through her numb hands. The world shifted into slow motion. A bitterly cold wind turned her vision blurry, making it difficult to make out the profile of the departing driver.

The back end of a vehicle had been smashed against the fuel pumps, leaving Captain Conner Gates wondering what had happened here. When Dispatch sent him on the hit-and-run call, he had expected to see a fender bender and two drivers arguing over who was at fault.

This was far more than a simple collision.

An uneasy feeling swept over him as he pushed open the door on the patrol car and climbed out. Despite having grown up in Quail Hollow, he'd never get used to the cold. Squinting against a blast of wind, he inspected the crumpled back end of the vehicle driven against the cement base of the fuel pumps. No sign of a second vehicle. Unease tightened like a fist in his gut. The images from the night of his cousin's fatal accident six weeks ago were seared into his brain. Well, technically, Jason was the son of a cousin, but he'd been like a brother to him. Jason's pickup truck had clipped an Amish woman's wagon then continued on, careening out of control and coming to rest wrapped around the solid trunk of a tree. Past experience told him no one could survive the brutal impact.

Past experience had been right.

Jason had died instantly.

Blinking away the graphic image of the young man's bloodied face, Conner muttered to himself that he hoped no one was injured tonight. He had long ago given up on prayer.

The dispatcher hadn't indicated any injuries.

Conner flipped up his collar and shrugged his shoulders against the punishing winds. The harsh glare of the emergency lights on his patrol car cut across his line of vision. He caught sight of a woman standing inside the minimart with a blanket wrapped around her shoulders. The woman next to her, Erin, the gas station clerk in her green uniform vest, waved at him frantically. Conner stopped at the minimart at least once a shift for some friendly chatter and hot black coffee.

He glanced around. There was only one other car in the lot, and it hadn't sustained any damage. He spoke into his shoulder radio. "I'm at the gas station. Send a tow truck." He yanked open the glass door and stepped inside. "You okay?" he asked the shivering woman. "Need an ambulance?"

Her red fingers flitted in a quick wave of dismissal. "No. No ambulance. I'm okay."

He nodded briefly and relayed the information to Dispatch.

Conner tugged off his leather glove and held out his hand. "I'm Captain Gates from the sheriff's department." Her hand was ice cold. "Can you tell me what happened here?"

"Someone rammed into my car and took off." Conner expected to hear fear in the woman's tone. Instead, he was met by the hard edge of annoyance. "It's my sister's car," she added, as if that might explain her tone.

"It was horrible." Erin rolled up on the balls of her orthopedic shoes and her eyes brightened with excitement. This was, after all, probably the most thrilling thing she'd witnessed in her fifty-odd years. "I've never seen anything like it. Always thought maybe someday someone would come crashing through the front of the store. You know?" She touched the arm of the woman standing next to her. If she had been looking for an ally, she didn't find one in the woman's steely gaze. The clerk continued, undeterred. "I see that all the time on the TV. But, wow, never seen anything like that in real life. He was aiming right for this lady's car."

"You saw the accident?"

"Yes," Erin said. "I looked up when I heard the tires squeal. At first I thought it was on account of the snow and ice. But no, this was *completely* intentional. He tried to crush her between the car and fuel pumps." The clerk's eyes grew wide. "I didn't catch the license plate. He pulled in and parked there shortly before this lady arrived. Never came into the store. I didn't think much of it because people use this parking lot all the time to shop at other stores. Easier than street parking."

"Did you notice anyone getting out of the truck?" Conner asked.

"Can't say that I did."

Conner directed his attention to the attractive woman who clasped a blanket tightly around her shoulders. Her attention was focused on the parking lot, or maybe her car. What was she searching for? "Any surveillance camera footage from that part of the parking lot?" Conner asked.

"Doubtful. You're free to look, though," Erin offered. "The only camera is pointed at the register."

"Do you…" He backed up his train of thought and turned toward the shivering woman. "I'm sorry. What's your name?" It wasn't often that he met strangers in Quail Hollow. It was one of those places where everyone knew everyone else or, at the very least, knew *of* everyone else. He most definitely had never met this brunette with watchful brown eyes. Yet something about her seemed vaguely familiar.

"Grace Miller." She blinked slowly, as if she had to think about it.

He made a mental note of it. Miller was a common Amish name around here; however, this woman was definitely not Amish. Not with her long brown hair flowing out from under her knit cap. Not to mention her expensive-looking boots, albeit not snow boots.

"Do you have ID?"

She held up her hand toward the smashed car. "My purse is on the passenger seat."

"No problem. We can deal with that later. Want to tell me what happened?"

A shadow crossed her eyes as if she were deciding how much to tell him. "I was pumping gas and some guy crashed into me. And took off." She seemed bored with the retelling. It was odd. Most people would have been completely panicked if someone rammed into their car while they pumped gas.

"Do you know the guy? Did you see him or get a license plate?"

"Of course I don't know him. And no, I didn't get a license plate. I was too busy diving out of the way." She twisted to get a better look at the slushy, black snow on her pants. She winced and her hand moved to her midsection. "I only saw a profile. Male. It was too hard to make out his face."

"Are you sure you don't need a doctor?"

"I'll be fine. I had my appendix out a few weeks ago. Landing on my side didn't do much for my recovery." Apparently sensing he was going to push the doctor thing again, she held up her hand. "I'm fine, really. I want to go home and change my clothes. I'm soaking wet."

"All right." Conner glanced around. The beeping sound of a tow truck backing up to her damaged car filled the night air. "Do you have someone you can call for a ride?"

"Um, no?" Her answer came out as a question. "I don't suppose Quail Hollow has Uber."

He suppressed a chuckle. "Let me take a few photos of the scene, talk to the tow truck driver, then I'll see that you get home."

A fraught expression tightened her pretty features. "That would be great."

"Wait here where it's warm."

Grace hugged the blanket closer around her and shuddered. "That's a matter of opinion." Her lips tilted into a weary smile, but he didn't miss the daggers shooting from her eyes.

For all the investigative journalism Grace had done over the years, she had never sat in the front seat of a patrol car. She had never sat in the backseat, either, for that matter. She'd come close a few times, but she had a knack for knowing when pushing law enforcement for answers had drifted from merely annoying to "let's lock her up."

The officer had started the engine, then

climbed back out of the vehicle. She felt a little guilty about being coy regarding what happened tonight. She hadn't *just* been filling her gas tank. She had come here because she had received a tip on the story she was working on. However, the sheriff's department had been less than forthcoming with information when it came to the underage drinking party and subsequent fatal car accident.

Two could play at that game.

Besides, she didn't want to become part of the story. If she kept her mouth shut, the hit-and-run would be a little blurb on the back page of a local paper and not part of a larger story, one that she was trying to cover. That was, *if* Quail Hollow had a newspaper.

Grace hadn't dealt with this officer from the sheriff's department before. Maybe she could pry some information out of him before he realized she was a journalist.

Just maybe…

Just maybe that would be unethical, a little voice whispered in her head.

Stifling a shiver, Grace adjusted the vent on the dash, glad the officer had turned on the heat before getting back out of his patrol car to talk to the tow truck driver and retrieve her purse from the passenger seat of her car. She plucked at the fabric of her wet pants, eager to get home and change.

When the officer finally climbed behind the steering wheel, he handed her the purse. "Warming up?"

"Thanks. Yeah."

"Before we go, I want to see if you recall anything else from the accident. Anything else important you haven't told me?" His intense brown eyes searched her face. She wasn't ready to talk. Not yet.

Twisting her lips, she shrugged. "Not really." She pulled on the blanket she was sitting on to smooth out the crease cutting into her thigh. "I'd love to get home and change out of these wet clothes."

He hesitated a moment then asked, "Where are you staying? Do you have friends or family in Quail Hollow?"

Grace couldn't resist smiling. This was small-town life. Since he hadn't met her before, she couldn't possibly belong in Quail Hollow. And he wasn't wrong. Grace doubted she'd ever fit in here, regardless of her background. "I'm staying at the bed & breakfast."

The fluorescent lighting from the gas station overhang lit on the handsome angles of his face. A look of confusion flickered in his eyes. "The Quail Hollow Bed & Breakfast? It's closed for the season. The owners…" He stopped himself, perhaps realizing it wasn't prudent for law enforcement to reveal when the residents of their fine town were away on an extended vacation.

"Yes, I know. My sister and Zach are on their honeymoon."

The officer's eyes widened, and he pointed at her with a crooked smile. "I knew you looked familiar. It was bugging me. Of course, your last name's Miller. A lot of Millers live around here." He put the patrol car in Drive. "Let me get you home."

"I'd appreciate that." She turned and watched the driver tow her sister's smashed-up car away on the back of the flatbed truck. So much for successfully taking care of things while her sister was away. Her stomach bottomed out, and a new worry took hold: it would require writing a lot of articles to pay for the damage. Her sister most likely had insurance, yet repairs still meant an inconvenience to everyone involved.

She pushed the thought aside. The occasional voice crackled over the police radio, interrupting the silence that stretched between her and the officer. Something about a deputy taking their dinner break and something else about Paul King's cows blocking the road and that someone was sure to have a wreck if the animals weren't cleared from the road right away. At that, she cut a sideways glance at the officer, who seemed unfazed. "Bet you're glad you got taxi duty and don't have to deal with the cows."

He laughed, a weary sound, as if he had heard it all before. "Oh, I'm sure I'll be dealing with the cows once I get you home."

"Are cows blocking the road a regular occurrence around here?" Maybe she could somehow work that into her article about the dark side of Amish life.

"We've been after Paul to get his fence repaired. These things take time, I suppose. It's all part of a slower-paced life."

Grace snagged her opening. "I heard there was some excitement in town about a month and a half ago."

The officer seemed to stiffen. He kept his eyes straight ahead on the country road. "That's the kind of excitement we don't need or want."

"I heard there was a big drinking party." She ran her hand down the strap of her seat belt, choosing her words carefully. "Is it unusual for the Amish and the townies to party together?" She had a hard time imagining her quiet father, who'd grown up Amish, drinking a Budweiser with his buddies out in some field.

The officer made an indecipherable sound. "The Amish and *Englisch* grow up together in some ways. They overlap in jobs and in the community. It *is* a small town. It's not unusual, especially during *Rumspringa*, for the Amish to test their limits." The Amish didn't encourage their youth to misbehave during this period of freedom prior to being baptized, but she understood the theory behind it. The Amish elders wanted their youth to willingly choose to be baptized into the faith after exploring the outside world. Surprisingly, a majority of Amish youth did decide to be baptized. It was a fact that had jumped out at her during her initial research.

Despite being the daughter of Amish parents, Grace had only recently started to research the Amish. There had been a reason she had avoided exploring her past. However, now she wished her father had opened up more about his Amish upbringing. It would make writing this story that much easier. But after her father had left Quail Hollow and the Amish way, bringing his three young daughters with him, he refused to talk about "life before." Even the good parts. It was all too painful. And how could she blame him, considering the way her mother had died?

Grace plucked a small pebble from her coat. "How is the Amish girl who was in the accident that night?"

"She's in a coma. Her prognosis is uncertain." His unemotional tone made it sound like he was reading from a list.

"That's horrible. And the driver of the truck…" Grace purposely left the sentence open-ended, despite knowing the outcome.

"Died at the scene." The officer's grip tightened around the steering wheel, and a muscle worked in his jaw.

His reaction made her realize something for the first time, and her pulse thrummed loudly in her ears. "Were you on duty that night?" She studied his reaction, sensing she was on the verge of learning something fresh she could use in her story. Deep inside, a sense of guilt niggled at her.

Using someone else's misfortune...

No, she was writing a story that needed to be told. A young man had partied and then recklessly crashed into an Amish wagon, most likely ruining a young woman's life. Grace's job was to bring light to stories that needed to be told. And she was good at her job. It allowed her to travel and be financially independent.

He cut her a sideways glance this time, before slowing down and turning into the rutted driveway of the bed & breakfast, which was covered in a fresh layer of snow. He shifted the patrol car into Park and turned to look at her. "Why didn't you tell me you were a journalist?"

Her stomach felt like she was riding a rollercoaster car that had plunged over a ten-story crest. However, there was nothing fun about this feeling.

Her go-to move was to feign confusion. "I'm..." She slumped back into the passenger seat, rethinking her plan of action. He knew. But how?

"Are you investigating the underage party?" he asked.

Without saying a word, Grace turned and stared up at the bed & breakfast in the darkness. The house gave off a lonely, unwelcoming vibe. She should have left on a light in the kitchen.

"Can you explain this?" The officer pulled a crumpled piece of paper from his pocket. It was the note from the anonymous source that she had left on the passenger seat of her sister's car. The officer must have found it when he retrieved her purse. For a fleeting moment, she wished she could disappear into the vinyl seat.

"Why didn't you tell me you were meeting someone at the gas station?" Captain Gates pressed. "Don't you think maybe this note and the accident are related?"

TWO

"Yes, I *am* a writer. I don't think the accident had anything to do with my job." Had it? The words sounded wrong in her ears the minute Grace said them, but she was committed to her denial, because acceptance that someone had tried to hurt her—*kill* her—would put a serious crimp in her research. The sheriff's department wasn't likely to let this go unchecked, and she wasn't foolish enough to make herself a target.

Grace traced a finger along the armrest on the patrol car door and stared at the house. The house that had once been her grandmother's hunkered in the winter night like a monstrosity from her past.

"Really?" Grace shifted to face Captain Gates, astonishment etched on his handsome features. "You get a note to meet at the gas station. No one shows up to talk to you, then a truck nearly pins you between the car and the pump. You don't see the connection?"

"Now that you put it that way." Grace tended to use humor to deflect. Had she really been that obtuse? No, she had simply shoved the obvious to the back of her mind. She tended to be single-minded in her focus, and she certainly wasn't going to allow some jerk to deter her from the story. She'd have to be more cautious, that was all.

"This is serious," the officer said.

Grace unfastened her seat belt. "I've dealt with far more dangerous situations covering stories all over the world. I can handle a punk in a truck. Besides, if he wanted to hurt me, he would have. His goal was to scare me." She didn't know who she was trying to convince.

"Did he?"

"No, don't be ridiculous. I mean, I'm not too happy about what happened tonight, but I'm not going anywhere." She scratched her head under the edge of her winter hat. "I can't imagine why he wanted to scare me in the first place. I'm trying to get more details about the party the night of the fatal accident. Readers will be fascinated to learn that Amish teens have the same issues as everyone else."

"Who have you spoken to already?" The officer shifted, and the seat creaked under his weight. She lifted her legs a fraction from the seat, the dampness adding to her ill temper. She didn't need to be a deputy to follow his train of thought. Someone in Quail Hollow wanted to put an end to her investigation.

"Bishop Yoder wasn't helpful when I tried to talk to him about the party. He assured me that anyone caught acting in an inappropriate manner would be dealt with accordingly. Then he shooed me along like I was some unwanted flu bug."

"The Amish prefer to live separate. They're not going to be receptive to anyone shining a light on something negative like this. Law enforcement and the Amish have a tenuous relationship, too. They deal with us only if they have to. That's why, when a journalist comes snooping around, it makes our job harder because the Amish shut down."

"I'm not snooping around." Grace resented the accusation. "I don't force anyone to talk to me if they don't want to. I ask questions. They either answer or they don't." She preferred when they did, of course. "I also stopped by the victim's house," she continued, laying out the names of all the people she had already tried to talk to.

"Katy Weaver?"

"Yes, her brother answered the door and asked me to leave. Out of respect, I did."

"Have you tracked down any of the teenagers from town who were at the party?" His tone changed subtly to one of genuine interest.

"Not yet. Any teenagers I've met claimed they weren't there. I had hoped maybe tonight, after getting that note, I'd find out more information."

She wrapped her chapped fingers around the door handle on the passenger side of the patrol car. "Listen, my pants are soaked. I'm freezing. I need to go inside."

Captain Gates pushed open his door, and the dome light popped on. She shot a glance over her shoulder at him. "You don't have to walk me to the door. I'm fine."

"You're not getting off that easy." His deep voice rumbled through her. Despite her frustration with the sheriff's department thus far, she wasn't sorry Captain Gates was going to escort her to the door. The surroundings were pitch dark in a way that can only happen in the country, far from civilization and light pollution. The memory of the truck barreling toward her flashed in her mind, and renewed dread sprinted up her spine.

The officer's hand hovered by the small of her back, and the snow crunched under their boots as they crossed the yard. Grace dug out the keys to the bed & breakfast and unlocked the back door leading into a mudroom adjacent to the kitchen. She turned around in the small, dark space to thank him, and was caught off guard when he stepped into the mudroom behind her.

She cleared her throat, debating if she should ask him to leave. "Thank you for the ride home. I'm really tired. I need—"

"Turn on a few lights. Change into dry clothes. We need to talk."

* * *

Conner made sure the windows and doors were secure on the first floor of the bed & breakfast. After he checked the last window, he turned around, surprised to find Grace watching him from the bottom stair with a determined look on her face. "I'll be fine. My sister has an alarm system."

It made sense. Heather Miller, Grace's sister, had been the target of a vicious stalker almost two years ago. Her ex-husband had escaped prison and found his way to Quail Hollow, where his former wife had hoped to start a new life. Thankfully, U.S. Marshal Zachary Walker had protected her, and duty had turned to love. Now the two of them were on their honeymoon. He wished them all the best. They seemed like a nice couple. He only hoped the challenges of a career in law enforcement didn't wreak havoc on their marriage like it had on his parents'.

He cleared his throat. "Can't hurt to check to make sure everything is locked up."

"Was it, Captain?" He detected a hint of sarcasm in her tone.

He lifted an eyebrow and couldn't hide his smile. Her cheeks were rosy from the weather. She stared back at him blankly. He could tell she was humoring him.

"Yes, everything was secure. Yet I don't like the idea of you out here all alone."

Grace's lips parted. "You're kidding me, right? Would you say that to a guy?" She glared at him, skepticism shining in her eyes. "I'm more than capable of taking care of myself. I don't need some big, strong law enforcement officer to protect me," she said in a singsong voice.

Conner had to consciously will the smile from his face, not wanting to stoke the flames of her anger. "I didn't mean to offend you. My job is to keep the residents of Quail Hollow safe. All of its residents, regardless of gender."

Grace dipped her head and ran a hand across her neck. She had twisted her long brown hair into a messy bun at the back of her head. She had also changed into gray sweatpants and a sweatshirt with the name of a university emblazoned across the front. He remembered the story his father had told him about how Grace's father had taken his three young daughters away from Quail Hollow after their mother was murdered. How different their lives had turned out. Grace would have never gone to college if she had been baptized into the Amish community. She'd probably be married with a few kids by now.

He shook his head, dismissing the image. "Are you warming up?"

"Yeah, let me throw another log into the woodstove. You said we needed to talk."

"Yeah." She opened the door and tossed in another log. The orange embers scattered and a new flame sparked to life. He feared if he offered to help her, she might bite his head off. She seemed the independent sort.

"How old were you when you moved away from Quail Hollow?"

She grabbed a second log and tossed it in. "Three," she said, without questioning how he knew her background. That seemed par for the course in Quail Hollow, especially since he knew her sister. Grace straightened with her back to him.

"My dad was the sheriff when your mother…" He scrubbed a hand across his face. As hardened as he had become over the years, this felt too personal to casually toss out the word *murdered*.

Grace slowly turned around. "I didn't know that. I haven't done much research on my mom's death." She frowned. "I only have vague recollections of her. My memories are a blend of my own and stories told by my oldest sister, Heather. She was six when my mom died." Then she seemed to mentally shake herself and held out her hand to one of the wooden rocking chairs in front of the wood-burning stove. "Have a seat. What did you want to talk about?"

"What is the focus of the story you're working on? Why were you meeting someone at the gas station?"

She slowly sat in the rocker next to his and unwound and rewound the fastener in her hair, as if stalling. The skeptic in him wondered if she'd tell him the truth.

She stopped fidgeting with her hair, placed her hands in her lap and angled her body toward him. "My editor asked me to cover the underage party and the fatal accident. The image of buggies lined up and police arresting the underage Amish drinkers has been splashed all over the news. My editor thought it made a fantastic visual. Like two eras intersecting." She held up her fingers in a square, framing the perfect shot. "Since I was already here recuperating from my surgery—" she shrugged "—it made sense for me to do a more in-depth story."

"Your surgery?" Then he remembered their conversation at the gas station. "Your appendectomy."

"Yes." She waved her hand in dismissal. "I'm fine. I'm still hanging around as a favor to my sister, keeping an eye on the bed & breakfast."

"I'm glad to hear it." He tapped his fingers on the arm of the rocking chair, deciding how to phrase his next question. "Did you ever think you'd have a much bigger story if you covered your mother's murder?"

She closed her eyes and tipped her head back on the chair. "I don't want to dig into that case. I like to keep my personal and professional lives separate." She opened her eyes and leaned forward. "Besides, that's old news." The haunted look in her eyes suggested otherwise.

Conner tapped his fist lightly on the arm of the rocker. The heat from the stove warmed his skin. "The case still haunts my dad."

Grace let out an awkward laugh, as if to say, "Yeah, it haunts me, too."

"I could set up an interview with him if you'd like. It doesn't mean you have to do the story. Maybe it'd provide some answers." He wrapped one hand around the other fisted hand and squeezed. "Truth be told, it might do my father some good to see that you turned out all right." His father often talked about the tormented look in the eyes of the three young Amish girls.

"Has your father ever talked to Heather?"

Conner shook his head. "From what I gather, she's forgiven the person who murdered your mom and has moved on. I'm guessing that's not the case with you." He wanted to ask about the youngest sister, but couldn't recall her name.

She shook her head quickly, but he wasn't sure what question she was answering. "My assignment is to write a story on the youth of Quail Hollow. The Amish. The drinking. The accident. Not something that happened almost thirty years ago." There was a tightness to her voice. "I hope you can understand, Captain Gates."

"Please, call me Conner. Otherwise I feel like we're in an interrogation room." He leaned forward and added, "I don't mean to add to your pain."

Grace smiled tightly. "No, not at all. That was a lifetime ago." She was obviously downplaying her emotions, and he regretted bringing up her mother's murder. No one ever got over losing their mother at such a young age. He still struggled with losing his mom, and she was still alive. After his parents got divorced, she married someone else and seemed perfectly content with her replacement family, never bothering to return to Quail Hollow.

He felt a quiet connection to this woman. Perhaps it was from remembering the impact her mother's murder had had on the entire community. Perhaps from the pain radiating from her eyes. He understood pain.

"I'm going to lay it on the line. I don't want you covering the story because Jason Klein, the young man killed in the accident, is—was—my cousin's son."

She sat back and squared her shoulders. "Oh… I'm sorry. I didn't know."

"My cousin and I were like brothers. When Ben, Jason's father, was deployed with the army last year, he asked me to keep an eye on his son. A teenager needs a male role model, you know? Anyway, Ben was killed in a helicopter crash."

Grace seemed to stifle a gasp. "I'm sorry."

"Thanks." Conner paused a moment, not trusting his voice. "Turns out, I did a lousy job of looking after his son."

"Kids make their own choices. It's not your fault."

"I don't want this one night—this one stupid, stupid decision—to be what Jason's forever remembered for. I need you to kill this story."

Grace slumped in the rocking chair and pulled her sweatshirt sleeves down over her hands, feeling like someone had punched her in the gut. "Wow, I'm sorry, but—" she bit her lip, considering her options "—I have to do this story. It's my job. I can't afford to lose my job."

Conner stared straight ahead at the woodstove, the flames visible through slots in the door. A muscle worked in his jaw.

"It's my livelihood. I've already begun posting little teasers on my blog about the story. If I don't follow through, it'll look bad." The words poured from her mouth, as if she were trying to convince them both that writing this story was the right thing to do.

When Conner didn't respond, she added, "I'm sorry for your loss, but what about the Amish girl in the hospital? Who gives her a voice? She's innocent in all this." Grace tempered her response out of respect for his loss.

"My cousin's wife, Anna, is having a terrible time with all this. She lost her husband and now her son. Jason was a good kid who made a horrible decision. More publicity only adds to the pain."

"He hadn't been involved with alcohol or drugs before that night?" Grace found her journalistic instincts piqued.

"Off the record?" Conner met her gaze.

"Yeah."

"A couple weeks before his death, Jason had a few friends over for a bonfire at his house after a big football game. Anna called me, worried that there might be some drinking going on. So I showed up, drove some guys home and Jason dealt with some blowback from that night. Apparently drinking is grounds for suspension from the football team. The star quarterback was one of the guys suspended. They're a pretty tight group. They weathered the storm and moved on. Kids make mistakes. Most importantly, no one was hurt that night. Anyway…"

The story angles swirled in Grace's head, making her dizzy. Was she really this insensitive? A good story above all else?

"Jason swore to me he wasn't drinking at his bonfire. That the other guys brought the alcohol. I had no reason not to believe him. I gave him the riot act, anyway. I thought that'd be enough." The inflection in his voice spoke of his pain far more than his words. Yelling at his cousin's son for hosting a drinking party wasn't enough to stop him from being killed a few weeks later in an accident where he was impaired.

"How do you explain the drugs in his system the night of the crash?" she asked hesitantly.

"I can't." Conner pushed up from his rocker and began to pace the small space in front of the stove. "He made a mistake. Must have taken something he didn't know how to handle. Doesn't mean he wasn't a good kid."

"This isn't about good kids and bad kids. It's about making decisions and suffering the consequences. Maybe some other kid will read the story and think twice before experimenting with drugs or alcohol. Perhaps the fact that he was a good kid will make a stronger impression. Show that it only takes one time." Grace stood and folded her arms across her chest. Heat pumped from the stove, but it barely touched the chill in her bones.

"I'm sorry about your loss," she continued, "but I'm sure the young Amish girl is a good kid, too." The fact that she had just met this man stopped her from reaching out, touching his arm, offering him comfort. "I hope you understand that I have a job to do."

He stopped pacing and stared down at her. "You realize, besides causing Jason's mother tremendous pain, you're also making it exceedingly difficult for the sheriff's department to find out who provided the drugs the night of the party?"

Offended, Grace jerked her head back. "How?"

"The more you go digging around, the harder you're making it for law enforcement to do the same. The Amish don't like to be in the spotlight."

"Maybe I provided you a lead tonight. Go find the truck that rammed my sister's car. Then you'll find someone who has something to hide."

"Trust me, we'll be working that angle. Meanwhile, I need you to stay put."

"Don't tell me to stay put." Anger surged hot and fiery in her veins. She didn't take commands from anyone, certainly not a man she had just met.

"I can't keep saving you if you're being reckless."

"I hardly think pumping gas is being reckless."

Conner held up his hand, then backed up. "Good night. Set the alarm when I leave." He pulled a business card from his pocket. "Here's my cell phone number. I'll respond quicker than a 9-1-1 call from a cell. Sometimes those calls are routed through a few substations before they can find the origin."

"If you're trying to scare me, you're not."

He set the card down on the table and looked at her intently. "I'm not trying to scare you. You need to understand how things are. Good night," he added tersely, turning to leave.

She stomped to the back door and turned the lock behind him. An ache in her hip from her heroic dive earlier this evening joined the dull pain from her appendectomy surgery.

The memory of the truck barreling toward her came to mind. She entered the alarm code and hit On, convincing herself she was safe. She had pursued far more dangerous stories in far scarier parts of the world. She wasn't afraid of some teenager in a souped-up truck, if indeed the accident at the gas station had been intentional.

She returned to the sitting room and slipped her laptop out of the case resting against her sister's fancy rolltop desk. She logged on to her blog, the one the editor encouraged her to keep updated. Since he was the one who assigned the stories, it was in her best interest to keep him happy.

"It gets the readers excited," he'd told her more than once.

She focused her thoughts, her fingers hovering motionless over the keyboard. The hurt and betrayal in Conner's eyes would haunt her. The dead boy had been his family. His responsibility.

The young man had made a horrible error in judgment that put a young Amish girl in a coma. People had to take responsibility for their actions.

No one had ever taken responsibility for her mother's murder.

She considered all the hurt and deceit in

her life. Her mother's murder. Her sister's violent husband. People weren't always who they seemed to be. She had to shed light on the evil of the world. Give victims a voice.

This was her job. Her editor expected her to write the story.

She clicked New Post and started to type:

The idyllic countryside is dotted with picturesque farmhouses and barns. The Amish people wear conservative clothing and use horses for transportation, as if living in another era. Yet the world changes around them at a dizzying speed.

Alcohol. Drugs. And other evils.

The Amish choose to live an insular life with porous borders that provide no barrier at all. They are warned to live separate from the world.

But, apparently, no one told the outsiders, for they have found a way in.

Grace drummed her fingers on the edge of the keypad and reread her words. Too dramatic?

She closed her eyes and tried to remember her mother's face. It was hazy, the memory of a three-year-old little girl.

Her mother had been murdered and no one had paid for the crime. Justice had never been served. Were the answers still out there? Was it really too late? What could it hurt to talk to the sheriff at the time of her mother's death? Could she still ask Captain Gates to set up a meeting with his father? She hadn't been very sympathetic to his family's plight when he asked her not to write about Jason.

Conner must think she was as cold as the winter winds slamming the outside walls of the Quail Hollow Bed & Breakfast. Nerves tangled in her stomach, and she made one more check of the alarm.

All set.

She wandered back to the seating area and stared over the yard. In the window, her weary reflection peered back at her. A chill raced down her spine.

She backed away from the window, unable to shake the sensation that she wasn't alone.

THREE

Late the next afternoon, after completing his shift, Conner strode around to the passenger side of his personal vehicle and opened the door for Grace. She had called him early that morning to see if the offer to talk to his father was still on the table. Conner considered this a good sign. Maybe they'd work out something mutually beneficial for both of them. She could get information on her mother's murder, and maybe she'd back off Jason's story.

When Grace didn't immediately unbuckle her seat belt, he asked, "Is something wrong?"

"Are you sure your dad's up for talking to me?"

"Yeah, come on. I called him earlier." He held out his hand, and she finally unbuckled her seat belt and slid out of the truck without taking it. "He generally doesn't like to discuss this case with outsiders, but that's not the situation here." Conner paused, not wanting to say that his father had always had a soft spot for the three little girls that Sarah Miller had left behind when she was brutally murdered. "He's willing to talk to one of Sarah's daughters.

"Besides—" he yanked open the back door and grabbed the takeout bags "—he's always up for food."

Grace held her scarf close to her neck as they walked up the pathway cleared of snow. Conner suspected his father had shoveled the flakes before they had a chance to hit the ground, whereas Conner preferred to put his four-wheel-drive truck to work each winter, creating two deep tracks in his long driveway. No shovel required. It was an ongoing joke between the two men.

"Watch out for the ice on the steps." The salt hadn't kept up with the sun-kissed icicles dripping from the overhang. He reached out for her elbow. She moved to the side and grabbed the railing instead.

"Any leads on the truck involved in the hit-and-run last night?" she asked.

"No, nothing on the surveillance video. But that was to be expected since it was positioned at the register and the driver never came into the store. All the officers know to look for a pickup with rear-end damage. If anyone tries to bring a truck in for repairs within a hundred-mile radius, we'll be notified."

Grace glanced up at him. "Why was it you

answered the call last night when you obviously work the day shift?"

Conner smiled. "It's a small town. I was filling in for another officer who requested off."

She nodded.

"I've also—" The door swung open, stopping Conner midsentence. His father must have been waiting on the other side for their arrival. "Hey, Dad."

"Son." The former sheriff stepped back into the foyer, allowing him and Grace to enter. His father took the takeout bag from his son before grabbing their coats with his other hand. He shuffled off to the first-floor bedroom where he undoubtedly placed the coats on the king-size bed, like Conner's mother used to do when they entertained when he was a little boy. It baffled Conner that, even after twenty-some years, the memory of his mother's habits made him miss her like the day she had left.

Time had passed. The Miller case had grown cold. His father retired. Yet his mother never returned, having found happiness with a nice engineer with regular hours and little chance of getting shot on the job. Apparently, the replacement kids meant she didn't miss the one she had left behind in Quail Hollow.

"Oh, something smells good." His father's voice snapped Conner out of his dark thoughts.

"Yeah, I picked up a few burgers from the diner," Conner said.

His father nodded. "This must be—"

"Grace Miller," Conner jumped in. "This is my father, Harry Gates."

His father narrowed his eyes, and a frown slanted his mouth. "If my memory serves me correctly, the Miller girls were Heather, Lily and Rose. Not Grace."

Conner watched Grace, wondering what that was all about. His memory had been a little hazy on the girls' names, but he hadn't given it much thought because she was staying at Heather's bed & breakfast. And the striking resemblance to her mother…

Had this woman deceived him?

Conner was starting to feel protective of his father when she finally spoke up. "I'm Lily. Lily Grace. I started going by my middle name when I went away to college." She smiled ruefully. "I wanted to put distance between my name and the tragedy that shaped my life."

"Seems reasonable," his father said without much ceremony. His father's career and failed marriage had hardened him. What little sentimentality that remained belonged to the family of Sarah Miller. The family he had let down.

"Regardless of the name, there's no doubt you're your mother's daughter. You have the same face." His father tipped his head. "However, she was Amish and you're—" he scanned her modern clothes and gave her a crooked smile "—obviously not. Do you see the resemblance yourself?"

"I only have a vague memory of my mom. The Amish don't allow photos, so I can only rely on my memories. I was only three when she died."

His dad held up his hand. "Of course. You were very young. Such a tragic thing. It's going on thirty years, isn't it?"

"Getting there. A lifetime ago." Conner detected a vulnerability in Grace that had been lacking last night when she was focused on his cousin's story. Perhaps she had been wise to keep her professional and personal lives separate.

Conner caught Grace's gaze briefly before his father invited them farther into the house. When they reached the dining room, Conner was surprised to see retired Undersheriff Kevin Schrock sitting at the table, his chair angled to keep an eye on some TV program with a guy haggling to buy some other guy's stuff. The big-screen TV dominated the adjacent family room. Kevin stood when they entered, and his dad was the first to speak. "I invited Kevin over. Kevin, this is Lil... Grace Miller. Grace, this is Kevin Schrock. He was one of the key investigators in your mother's case."

Grace shook his hand. "Thank you for taking the time to meet with me."

Kevin studied Grace's face, probably seeing the same thing that Conner's father saw: the likeness to the woman whose murder they had never been able to solve.

His father peered into the paper bag with blossoming grease stains on the bottom and sides. "Any chance you have an extra burger in here?"

"Of course." Conner pulled out a chair for Grace to sit down. "Plenty of food for everyone." He smiled at Kevin. "Nice to see you."

"Same here." Kevin picked up the remote sitting on the table in front of him and muted the TV program. He shifted in his chair to face Grace. "Boy, you certainly don't look like the little girl who left Quail Hollow in an Amish bonnet and bare feet."

Conner shot Kevin a stern look. These old-timers got directly to the point.

"I suppose not," Grace said softly.

"You've come back to find answers?" Kevin pressed, seemingly intrigued.

"That wasn't my intention. Not initially. I was staying at my sister's bed & breakfast for other reasons, and then my editor asked me to write a story regarding the underage drinking party involving both the Amish and the townies."

His father muttered something he couldn't make out, anger blazing in his eyes. He cleared his throat and finally spoke. "I'm sure my son told you that Jason Klein, the boy killed in the crash that night, was family."

Grace swallowed hard. "I'm sorry for your loss."

His father's expression grew pinched, and he faced Conner. "She's a journalist? I hadn't realized that."

"She wants to know about her mom."

Resting his elbows on the table, his father leaned forward. "If your motive is to drag poor Jason's name through the mud…" He shook his head. "Jason's mother has been through enough, hasn't she? First losing her husband in a horrible helicopter crash, now her son."

"That's not my intention, sir." Grace moved to sit on the edge of her seat. "I like to shed light on untold stories. I'm sure people would be fascinated to learn of the—" she seemed to be choosing her words carefully "—things that go on in an Amish community beyond farming and cross-stitch."

"You really did move away from here young." Kevin folded his arms, a self-satisfied look on his face. "The Amish do far more than farm and needlework."

Grace tucked a long strand of hair behind her ear. "I don't identify with the Amish at all. My father raised us in Buffalo. Please forgive me if I find this story fascinating. Others will, too. I'm sure of it."

"Oh, people will find it interesting," his father said. "They were all over your mother's murder, too."

Grace's face burned red, and uncertainty glistened in her eyes.

"Dad!" Conner scolded him. "Grace came here to talk, not to be put on the spot." Conner suspected his father's blunt comment was a result of wanting to protect Jason, his great-nephew.

"After your mother's murder, a young reporter thought she'd make a name for herself and wrote story after story about the Miller murder for the *Quail Hollow Gazette*. She inserted herself to the point that the Amish wouldn't talk to anyone anymore, not even law enforcement." His father fisted his hands in his lap, his anger evidently directed at a long-ago slight, not at the need to protect Jason. "The journalist was a huge detriment to our investigation."

"You never told me that." Conner studied his father's face. A vein throbbed at the elderly man's temple, his ire still palpable. His father had pored over paperwork and reports at the kitchen table long after the town had written Sarah Miller's death off to a tragic and random encounter with a stranger passing through town. Yet they had never been able to prove it.

Conner himself had never felt the need to read the newspaper accounts because the case had taken over his young life, leaving his father obsessed and his mother absent. Now, as a law enforcement officer, he understood the delicate relationship with reporters *and* with the Amish. He had recently tried to mind this relationship when he'd asked Grace to stop asking questions about the night Jason was killed.

"People would say my accusations regarding the reporter were only conjecture on my part," his father continued. "That *I* needed to take responsibility for not handling the investigation. That *I* was the only one responsible for not finding the murderer."

"My intention wasn't to upset you." Grace pushed back from her chair, stood and smiled sympathetically. "I'm sorry, sir. I was under the impression that your son had told you I was coming."

"He did. But I thought I'd be talking to Sarah Miller's daughter. Not a journalist."

"Please, sit down." Conner gently touched Grace's wrist and they locked gazes. He gave her a quick nod as if to say, "It's okay. Please stay." Trusting him, she sat down. If she hoped to learn anything about her mom, she didn't see that she had much of a choice.

She glanced over at the undersheriff. Tingles of awareness prickled her skin from the retired officer's intense focus. She hadn't realized she'd be ambushed when she arrived here.

"I'm sorry you had a bad experience with a reporter. I have no intention of making anyone look bad." Her only motivation was to reveal the truth. Let the rest of the chips fall where they may.

The retired sheriff grumbled under his breath, perhaps understanding more than most how these things worked.

Grace picked up a French fry and distractedly dipped it into the glob of ketchup she had squirted onto her paper plate. "I understand you put a lot of time into my mother's case. Why was this one more difficult than most?" She knew from her journalism career that all cases weren't neatly wrapped up.

Conner's father folded the corner of the takeout wrapper from his hamburger. "Murder is rare in Quail Hollow. Some might say I *was* out of my depth. I worked that case harder than I'd ever worked anything before. Or since." There was a faraway quality to his voice. "The best lead we had was a man who had been traveling through town. Eventually, we tracked him down, but he had a solid alibi. Rumors cropped up that there was another stranger in town. The locals needed to believe it was an outsider. It grew harder and harder to separate fact from fiction. But that's where we still are all these years later. A vagrant passing through town killed Sarah Miller."

"Were there any other suspects?"

The two retired law enforcement officers exchanged a subtle glance that she might have missed if she hadn't been so observant. A heaviness weighed on her chest, making the room feel close. When neither of them answered, she pressed, "What aren't you telling me?" A cold pool of dread formed in the pit of her stomach. *"What?"*

Kevin drummed his fingers on the table. She guessed it was a nervous habit. "In a murder investigation, the person closest to the victim is usually investigated."

She tossed aside the French fry and wiped her hands on a napkin. "That's not unusual." She shrugged, trying to act casual when her insides were rioting. *Her sweet father.* Her mother's murder had destroyed him. "You cleared my father and then moved on to this stranger passing through Quail Hollow." Her gaze shifted between the two men. Holding her breath, she waited for reassurance. *Of course* they'd cleared her father. Hadn't they?

Kevin finished chewing a bite of his burger and swallowed. "Your father moved out of town before we could one hundred percent clear him."

"Well, that's only partially true." Harry leaned forward and gave her a reassuring smile. "I knew your father a bit from town before your mother's murder. Your father and mother used to sell corn at the farmers market on the weekends. He was a friendly man. Talkative. You girls were his little helpers. After your mother's murder, he shut down. Her death broke him." He pressed his lips together. "Even though we never officially cleared him, my gut told me that he could never have hurt Sarah. *Never.*"

A lump of emotion clogged her throat. "Thank you." She averted her gaze, fearing she'd lose it if she didn't. This was the price of looking into her family's story, the reason she had avoided it all these years. The reason she'd probably leave here today and forget she ever came.

"What else can you tell Grace about the time surrounding her mother's death?" Conner asked the question Grace was now afraid to, because she was uncertain she could afford the emotional toll.

"The night Sarah disappeared, she had taken the horse and wagon into town to drop off a few pies. She had sold them to the diner. She left you girls home with your grandmother. A few people noticed her in town, but didn't see anything or anyone suspicious. She never came home."

She never came home.

Pinpricks of dread washed over Grace's scalp as if she were reliving her mother's last moments. She had vague memories of hanging out at the farmers market. Maybe the memories had been dreams, yet the images were vivid: the long dresses of the Amish women, the farmers' work boots and the fancy shoes of the *Englisch.* The occasional dog would lick her sticky fingers after she devoured a piece of apple strudel. The farmers' market was the highlight of the week. She figured the only reason she had those memories was because of how quickly her life had changed.

Amish to outsider.

Before versus after.

Conner's father glanced over at his former co-worker. "Anything else to add?"

"No. Not really. It was a shame we never found the guilty party. It was like he vanished into the night."

"You mentioned a reporter at the time..." Grace watched the former sheriff flinch.

"Yeah," Harry said. "She worked for the now-defunct *Quail Hollow Gazette*. She was like a dog with a bone. Relentless."

"Do you know if she still lives in Quail Hollow?" Grace asked, hope blossoming. Another piece of the puzzle.

Can I really do this?

Kevin leaned back and crossed his arms over his chest. "Can't be sure. I believe she had some health issues and moved away to live with her daughter down south. Away from this cold."

"I imagine they have her articles on file at the library," Grace said, thinking out loud. "Maybe I'll do some digging."

After they finished eating, Grace and Conner carried the paper plates and glasses into the kitchen. Grace leaned on the counter while Conner put the glasses in the dishwasher. "I'm not sure I'm ready to look into my mother's murder."

Conner slowly closed the dishwasher door and turned to face her. "Your mother's sudden death had to be really tough on you. Leaving this community must have made it that much harder."

"I often wondered how my life would have been if I had grown up Amish. I look at the Amish men and women in town and try to imagine the path not taken. Sometimes I wonder if this was all part of God's bigger plan." Heat crept up her face. "Don't get me wrong—I'd do anything to have my mom back. Yet no one could have predicted how her death changed everything about my life. Not all of it bad." She slowly ran a hand through her hair. "That sounds horrible, doesn't it?"

"No, life's twists and turns are hard to understand sometimes." He took a step closer to her, and she didn't move. "But some tragedies don't have any redeeming qualities."

"You're talking about Jason's death."

He nodded, a flash of hurt in his eyes. "I'm asking you not to continue to write about the death of my cousin's son. It's hard for our family, especially his mom. She lost her son and her husband in the course of a year. She's spiraling out of control. She's distraught."

A knot twisted in Grace's stomach. "I'm sympathetic. I really am, but you can't compare the two cases. Jason drove under the influence. *He* made a choice." She shifted away from the counter and glanced out the back window overlooking the snow-covered yard. The evening light was about to fade. "This is my job." Grace wondered how many times they'd go round and round on this topic.

"Everyone has a job to do." Grace spun around to find Kevin Schrock resting his shoulder on the doorway of the kitchen. "And sometimes it's best not to mix business with personal." How long had he been eavesdropping?

Kevin seemed unfazed that he had interrupted their private conversation. "His dad allowed your mother's case to get to him. Ruined his marriage." He pushed off the doorway and strolled into the room. "You have to trust your gut on these things. If you don't think you can live with what you find, maybe it's a story better left untold."

Grace stared at him, wondering which story he thought was better left untold.

A few days later, since her sister's car was still in the collision shop, Grace called the number for a car service in town. The Amish often hired drivers to get them from place to place when taking a horse and buggy wasn't feasible. The local district's *Ordnung* allowed the Amish to ride in the vans, but they couldn't own cars or drive themselves.

The driver, an older gentleman, dropped Grace off at the local library and promised to return in one hour to bring her home. Grace climbed out of the van and smiled at an Amish woman hustling past with three young daughters in tow. The thick fabric of their bonnets kept their heads warm. Their long dresses poked out from under black coats. The fabric brushed the edge of the shoveled walkway, collecting clumps of snow. Nostalgia pricked the back of Grace's eyes. Another generation ago, that could have been her and her sisters.

Grace held her collar closed and strode toward the main entry of the quaint library. Ever since retired Sheriff Gates had mentioned the articles in the *Quail Hollow Gazette* about her mother's murder, Grace couldn't get them off her mind. She tried Googling and using some of her research tools to find the articles online, but came up empty. At first, Grace took it as a sign that she needed to let the past stay in the past.

Her initial curiosity had been followed by a restless night and a growing determination that hollowed out the pit of her stomach. Grace hadn't become a top-notch reporter by allowing a dead end to stop her.

After alternating between "let it go" and "just read the articles already," she decided only the latter would allow her to move on. Besides, there couldn't be much to go on in the articles since no one had ever been arrested. Grace needed to squelch her obsessive curiosity, a quality that usually served her well.

She carefully made her way up the salt-covered walkway. She entered the library and drew in a deep breath. The smell of books filled her nose. Something felt familiar. Grace had always loved to read, and she wondered if perhaps her mom had brought her here. Instilled in her a love of reading.

Or maybe that had come later, growing up in Buffalo.

Grace approached the librarian. "Where can I find articles from the *Quail Hollow Gazette*?"

"Oh, the *Gazette* went under—" she hesitated, giving it some thought "—fifteen years ago."

"Do you have copies of the paper from the 1990s?" Grace didn't want to tell the librarian exactly what she was looking for because she didn't want to invite questions.

"We have clippings of the more important articles from the paper filed chronologically in the basement." The librarian emphasized the word *basement*, apparently trying to dissuade her.

"Is the basement open for patrons to do research?"

The librarian planted her hands on the desk and pushed to her feet. "Um, Linnie, I'm going to show this woman where the archives are in the basement," she said to her colleague, also behind the desk.

"Thank you," Grace said, hoping her gratitude would make the woman feel like her trouble was worth it. She had met all kinds during her travels, from those eager to tell her their life story, to those who seemed bothered by the idea of doing their job. Yet in Grace's experience, whatever her reception, she chose to be pleasant. It proved to be disarming—most of the time.

The librarian muttered something as she led Grace down a back hall marked with an overhead exit sign. She moved surprisingly quickly despite her short, choppy steps and the narrow purple dress she wore. She stopped at a door before the emergency exit. With the key on a lanyard around her neck, the librarian unlocked the door, reached in and flipped on the lights. "I'll show you the files, and then I have to get back upstairs to help Linnie. The library gets busy in the afternoon with all our after-school programs." She squared her shoulders with a sense of pride.

"That's fine." Grace preferred to do her research without anyone standing over her shoulder, anyway.

The fluorescent lights buzzed to life in the basement. The librarian led her down the stairs, past a row of shelves stacked with books with identical bindings to a series of gray filing cabinets along a cement wall. The librarian planted her hand on the top of the cabinet, then pulled it away and swiped her hands together. "It's a little dusty down here. Most libraries have this information on microfiche or digital but, well, we don't have the budget for that."

"I understand." Grace hoped her cheery yet sympathetic tone was effective. She didn't know how long she'd be here or if she'd need to come back, and she wanted the librarian on her side.

The woman clasped her hands in front of her. "What dates are you looking for?"

The filing cabinets were neatly labeled with month, day and year ranges. As long as the newspaper clippings were filed correctly according to date, she'd be able to search the articles at the time of her mother's murder. She touched the handle of the closest cabinet. "I see the files are labeled. I'll be fine."

"Well—" the woman pursed her lips "—don't refile anything. Place any files you pull out on the desk over there. I'll refile them at a later date. Because if you don't put them in the right spot—"

"No one will ever be able to find the article they're looking for in the future."

The woman leaned back on her heels, apparently satisfied. "When you're done, let me know. I'll be at the information desk upstairs."

"Thank you." Grace watched the librarian walk down the narrow aisle, the bookshelves lining one side and the filing cabinets the other, her heels clacking on the cement floor. The librarian disappeared around the corner, and Grace waited until she heard the basement door click shut.

Finally alone, Grace ran her fingers along the labels on the drawers and stopped on October of that fateful year. Her knees grew weak, and a darkness crowded the periphery of her vision. Was she about to open Pandora's box?

Should she or shouldn't she?

Drawing in a deep breath, she slid open the first cabinet drawer. She'd come this far. She'd check out a few articles, that's all. Inside the drawer, manila folders were labeled with exact dates. She slid out the folders from a few days before to a few weeks after her mother's body was found. She carried the stack to a desk at the far end of the aisle, pulled out a chair and sat. She squinted up at the flickering overhead lights, wishing there was a desk lamp. Not many people must use the basement.

She opened the folder dated the day after her mother's body had been found.

Amish Woman Found Dead.

Her mother's life had been reduced to a four-word headline. No name. Simply "Amish Woman."

The black words on the yellowed paper swam

in her field of vision. Blinking, she traced the letters, as if it provided a connection to her mother.

As she slowly read the article, she imagined the writer, fingers flying over the keyboard, jazzed to write about something more substantial than cows escaping through broken fences. A quiver rippled through her stomach. Was she any different?

She shook the thought away and focused on the article. It didn't provide any significant information that she hadn't already known. Her mother had gone into town to sell pies. The waitress oozed with pleasantries on how wonderful a person Mrs. Miller had been and then digressed into the usual platitudes: what an awful tragedy, her poor daughters, how had someone dumped her body in the family barn without being seen? It was almost too much to read.

Breathing slowly through her nose, Grace tried to calm her nerves. She pulled out another article and squinted at the black-and-white photo taken from a distance. Was that her with her father and sisters? The hairs on her arms prickled to life. Her grandma's house—the site of her sister's bed & breakfast before it had been updated—stood in the background. She recognized the tree out front and the porch. Emotions she wasn't ready to explore coursed through her.

The buzzing and winking of the yellow fluorescent lights threatened to trigger a migraine.

She slid the files into her tote bag, convinced the lighting would be better upstairs. She went over to the cabinet to close the drawer when the lights went out.

Her heart nearly exploded out of her chest.

Just great.

Frozen in blackness, Grace called out, "Hello, I'm down here."

The only response was the uneven sound of her breath.

"Hel-lo?" Her voice hitched. She didn't dare move for fear she'd trip over something in the blackness.

A muffled shuffling sent terror pulsing through her veins. "Hello? Is someone else down here?" She slid along the cabinets, the handles jabbing her side.

Hope made her change direction. Her phone was in her bag on the desk. It had a flashlight app. Or she could call for help.

A rhythmic creaking filled her ears, made louder in the blackness.

What is that?

"I'm down here!" she hollered in desperation.

"I know you're down here," an unseen man whispered. Tiny pinpricks of fear blanketed her scalp. She slid closer to the desk, realizing whoever was here had intentionally turned off the lights. And was coming for her.

Her hand found her tote bag on the desk. She

reached inside and found her phone. She feared pulling it out and revealing her location, but she needed help. She swallowed hard. *Remain calm. You've been in far scarier situations.* Her usual response to those who warned her that her investigation was going to get her into trouble didn't seem to be doing her much good at this exact moment.

A loud, rhythmic creaking filled her ears. A groan of exertion cut through the blackness. She scrambled under the desk with her phone.

A loud crash exploded in her ears. A violent whoosh of air sent her hair flying off her face.

The bookshelves had crashed down around her, leaving her trapped underneath the desk.

FOUR

Conner braced himself against the cold winter blast as he strode toward his patrol car, careful to avoid oncoming traffic. He had let the teenage driver in her mother's minivan off with a warning, mostly because he believed her when she told him through sobbing hiccups that she hadn't been able to stop at the icy intersection. He told her it was a good thing he'd been the one to pull her over, because the sheriff had given all his officers a directive to crack down on all driving offenses, especially among the youth. And, more importantly, it was a blessing that her slide into the intersection hadn't resulted in a crash.

Everyone needed to slow down and be more careful on the roads.

Safely back inside his warm patrol car, he balanced his clipboard on the center console and entered the information into the laptop. A little less paperwork for the end of his shift, which he was looking forward to more than usual. He thought he'd stop by and check on Grace. It had been a few days since he had seen her. He had convinced himself his visit was to make sure she wasn't getting herself into trouble, not because the spunky reporter had caught his attention. Not that he was looking for anyone to catch his attention.

But she had.

His cell phone buzzed and he glanced at the screen. He smiled to himself and swept his finger across the screen.

"Hello, Grace." Conner wasn't sure what he had expected when he picked up the phone. But it wasn't what he heard next.

"Conner." Her panicked voice was barely above a whisper. "Conner, can you hear me?"

"Yes." He pressed the phone to his ear, fearing he wouldn't be able to hear her over the sudden surge of adrenaline pulsing through his veins. "What's wrong?"

"I'm in the basement of the library. I'm trapped."

Conner glanced over his shoulder to check for oncoming vehicles and pulled out onto the road. "I'm a block away. Are you hurt?"

"No… I don't think so…" Her voice cracked. "But I'm trapped. Someone was down here."

"I'm on my way." He flipped on his lights and siren. He punched his foot down on the accelerator. Silence stretched across the phone line. "Grace? Are you there?"

Silence.

He eased off the gas as the library came into view. He scanned the crowded parking lot and realized his only option was to make his own spot. His patrol car bumped over the curb and came to an abrupt stop on the snow-covered lawn of the library. With the patrol car lights still flashing, Conner jumped out of the vehicle and sprinted across the lawn, the snow crunching under his boots. He flung open the library doors. He forced himself to slow down to avoid barreling into a couple of toddlers who had escaped from the not-so-watchful eye of their adult. The pair were now making a break for it, hand in hand, toward the group of senior citizens in the newspaper section.

A thin woman in a purple dress with black-frame glasses and hair twirled in a bun was the first to make eye contact with him. She scooted out from behind the information desk. If he hadn't been in such a panic to find Grace, it would have registered that the woman making a beeline for him with her pinched expression could have been plucked out of central casting for librarians.

"Officer, is there an emergency?" She angled her head to look around him, toward the wall of windows, no doubt to his patrol car parked on the front lawn, complete with lights flashing. Once he collected Grace, he'd make it up to the librarian by scheduling a date to give the kids a peek at a real patrol car.

"Where's your basement?" He strode toward the back of the library and looked both ways. He continued down the hall, proceeding on a hunch.

The librarian chased after him with choppy steps. "What's going on, sir? A woman is doing research in the basement. We have old records stored down there."

"Here?" Conner pointed at the door, then turned the handle. It was locked.

The librarian nodded and flattened her hand over a key on a lanyard around her neck. "Yes, it's usually locked, though it shouldn't be now." A line marred the woman's pale forehead, and Conner had to resist the urge to yank the key from around her neck—*now.* "Like I said, a woman is doing research down there."

"Open the door," he said through gritted teeth.

The librarian hunched over and stuck the key into the lock without removing the lanyard from around her neck. She opened the door and took a step through the opening. Conner held up his hand. "No. Wait here. Keep anyone else from entering this back hallway."

"Oh." The woman's eyes widened underneath her thick lenses.

Conner pulled out his gun, reached in and flipped on the basement light. The darkness scurried into the far corners where he couldn't see. Where someone could easily hide.

The wooden stairs creaked under his cautious step. Grace was in the basement. He had no idea if she was alone.

A cramp shot up Grace's leg. It had been twisted under her for what seemed like forever, in a position no amount of exercise could have prepared her for. Pressing her eyes closed, she held the phone tight to her chest. She didn't dare talk more than she had to for fear of revealing her location.

She whispered a prayer of thanks when she heard the sound of a siren growing closer. Conner really had been close by. Her solace was short-lived when she opened her eyes and realized it was just as dark as when she had them pressed closed. A memory slammed into her, unbidden, and ramped up her panic.

It was a long time ago. Grace was a teenager. Heather, her eldest sister, had come home after a big fight with her new husband. Grace loved having her sister around, and they had spent a fun evening watching a movie and eating popcorn. Their other sister, Rose, had been at a sleepover at a friend's house. The credits for one of their favorite movies had begun to roll when Heather's husband, Brian, pounded on the door looking for "his woman." At the sound of his banging—his yelling—all the color drained from her sister's face. The woman Grace looked up to, admired, the big sister who had always protected her two little sisters in their mother's absence, had a sheen of terror in her eyes that shook Grace to her very core.

Heather grabbed Grace roughly by the shoulders and shoved her toward the front hall closet. Before Grace knew what was happening, she was curled up among the shoes, umbrellas and whatever stuff she had thrown in there the last time she'd quickly cleaned up.

Grace remained in the closet until the shouting stopped and the police took Brian away. Heather never took refuge in her childhood home again, because she knew that she'd be putting her little sisters' lives in jeopardy.

A rustling, then a snap sent light filtering from the far end of the basement and brought Grace immediately back to her current predicament. The fallen bookshelves in the basement of the library came into fuzzy focus in the dim lighting. Grace swallowed back the urge to call out. What if it wasn't Conner?

Dear Lord, help me.

She'd give up the scoop on the next big story in a tropical climate just to be able to stretch out her legs again. She tried to shift to ease the pain and bumped her head on the underside of the desk.

Ugh. Time had dulled the fear and now she

was frustrated. Annoyed. She angled her head and strained to see toward the stairs to determine who was coming down.

Footsteps sounded on the stairs, then legs came into view. She squinted. Uniform pants?

Emboldened by her certainty that Conner was here, she stretched out a hand and pushed the side of the metal shelving. It wouldn't budge.

She flashed back to the memory of being stuck in the front hall closet. Brian screaming at her sister. Heather crying.

An overwhelming sense of claustrophobia swept over Grace. She needed to get out of this confined space *now*.

"I'm over here! Get me out of here!" she screamed.

Grace pivoted and scraped her back on the underside of the desk. Ignoring the pain, she shoved with all her strength against the metal shelving with two hands. The metal scraped against the cement floor.

"Grace! Hold up!"

She sat back on her feet, her entire upper body hunched over to fit under the space of the desk. Her elation at seeing Conner overwhelmed her.

"Are you okay?" he asked.

She held up a hand to block the beam from his flashlight. "Yes. Now please get that light out of my eyes." Her panic made her irritable, and she suspected he'd use this against her. She'd heard the words countless times before from other well-meaning acquaintances. *Investigating this is too dangerous. You need to stop.*

But whatever happened here this afternoon only proved she was on to something important. Something she had to continue to investigate.

"Keep your limbs under the desk. I'm going to shove the shelving out of the way."

After some grunting and tossing books aside, Conner made a space big enough to reach her. "Grab my hand."

Grace slid her hand inside his solid one, and immediately the panicky feelings subsided. He started to pull her through the gap between the fallen shelving and the desk, when she squeezed his hand. "Hold up." She ducked back under the desk and slid the strap of her tote over her shoulder.

Grace found his hand again and let him pull her to safety over a stack of fallen books and mangled shelving. Once free and on solid ground, he held her out at arm's length. "You okay?"

Suddenly self-conscious, she pulled her hand from his and swiped at the back of her pants. She shook both legs to stretch them out. "I am now. My legs were falling asleep under there."

Conner glanced around, a muscle working in his jaw. "What happened?"

She tucked her elbow closer to the tote hanging from her arm. "I came down here to do some research and next thing I know, the lights go out, I'm under the desk, and the shelves come crashing down."

"Did you see anyone?"

Grace shook her head, thinking back to the pitch darkness. "It was a male voice. He said something like, 'I know you're here' or 'down here.'"

"Did you notice anyone following you today?"

"No, of course not." Grace's fear had morphed into indignation as she struggled to process what had happened. "Do you think I'd come down here alone if I thought someone was following me?"

"What happened down here?" The librarian had found her way to the bottom of the stairs and was clutching the lanyard at her neck as she took in the mess. Her eyes slowly shifted to Grace. "Are you okay?"

"I'm fine. Thank you. And about this..." She held up her palm to the mess. "I can help you put everything back in place."

The librarian shook her head. "No, no. We'll have to make sure everything is filed correctly." She rubbed her nose. "Maybe Linnie... Oh, dear." She shook her head and tut-tutted. Grace could see this woman reacting the same way to teenagers talking too loud in the quiet section of the library. "I've been so busy training Linnie. And then this…"

"I'm very sorry," Grace said.

Conner touched her arm. "You don't need to apologize. You didn't do this."

The librarian opened her mouth, but Conner cut her off before she had a chance to protest. "Did you see anyone who looked out of place in the library?"

One of the librarian's eyebrows drew down above the frame of her glasses. "We welcome everyone to our library. We don't—"

"I understand." Conner took a deep breath. "But did anyone stand out today? Someone who looked like they had the strength to knock over this shelving unit? Someone who usually doesn't come to the library?"

Grace leaned toward Conner. "I have to get out of here." Even though she had escaped her tiny hidey-hole under the desk, the basement felt like a tomb. She smiled meekly at the librarian and tried to ignore the sweat dripping down her back. "I have to get air."

Conner nodded at Grace and guided her out of the basement with a hand on her lower back. They left the librarian in the basement to assess the damage with a warning not to touch anything. Not yet. He'd have to send a crew over to see if they could get fingerprints or any other evidence.

When they reached the top of the stairs, Grace

pointed to the door to the right of the basement door. "Anyone could have run out through the exit."

Conner moved toward the door, keeping her safely tucked by his side. "There's a single track of footsteps in the snow headed toward the parking lot."

A cold chill skittered down her spine that had nothing to do with the swirl of snow flitting over the top of the lawn.

Someone had tried to kill her.

"I'm fine, *really*. Thanks for bringing me home." Grace stopped in the back doorway of the bed & breakfast, seeming eager for Conner to leave.

Conner placed his hand on the frame of the door. "We need to talk. I promise I won't stay long."

Grace's eyes lit up, then she turned to hang her tote on a hook inside the door. "Oh, you mean in an official capacity. You need to fill out your reports." He detected a hint of something in her tone. Yeah, he wasn't too thrilled about the reports, either.

"Yeah, reports." He smiled and shrugged. "The reason I got into law enforcement was because I love paperwork."

Grace's strained expression softened and a tired giggle escaped her lips. "Come in."

Conner slid off his snow-covered boots. He took off his hat and hung it on an empty hook. He could imagine the Amish men who had lived here a generation ago coming in from their chores and hanging their wide-brimmed hats on similar hooks in the entryway.

Grace busied herself in the kitchen. "Want some tea? Or coffee? I only have instant coffee," she added with a hint of apology. "I'm not much of a coffee drinker."

Conner waved his hand. "I'm fine. Don't bother yourself on my account. I need to get a full report of what happened today."

Grace finished filling the teakettle and set it down on the stovetop, but stopped short of turning on the burner. She turned around and leaned her backside against the counter and crossed her arms, not exactly looking receptive. "I don't know any more than I already told you. I went into the library basement to do research, and someone turned off the lights and knocked over the shelves."

Conner leaned his shoulder against the fridge. "You sure you didn't notice anyone suspicious following you?" She shook her head. "Did anyone know you were going to the library?"

She glanced up with a thoughtful look in her warm eyes. "Only the ride service I hired to drive me into town." A weariness had settled in around her eyes.

Conner ran the back of his hand over his mouth and levered off the refrigerator with his shoulder. "Can I ask you something?"

Grace blinked slowly, exhaustion evident on her face. "I've told you everything already."

Realizing Grace was shutting down, he tried to shift the mood. "I thought this B&B was supposed to be an authentic Amish experience."

"Um, yeah?" Grace looked up, her fatigue replaced by curiosity.

Conner jabbed his thumb toward the refrigerator. "Why do you have a fridge in here?"

Grace shook her head, and a smile pushed at the corners of her mouth. "I don't know. I suppose because it's convenient. I'm just housesitting. What does that have to do with anything, anyway?"

He took a step toward her. "You look serious. I thought maybe I could get you to smile. And I think I did. A little, maybe?"

Grace removed her ponytail and threaded her fingers through her hair, kneading her scalp. "I've had a really, really rough day, and even the muted light from the wall sconces that are, in fact, Amish approved, are hurting my eyeballs."

"Okay, then, I'll make it quick." He slipped the tote from the hook and offered it to her. Apprehension stole across her otherwise bland expression, confirming his suspicions. "What's in the bag?"

Grace's chin dipped as if she were carefully studying the floor.

"Grace," he said quietly, and that caught her attention.

She took the tote from him and their fingers brushed in the exchange. "I'll show you."

She carried the tote to the table next to the windows overlooking the yard and a gorgeous newly constructed barn. The Amish neighbors had all pitched in and had a barn raising to replace the one that had burned down in a horrific fire that nearly killed Grace's sister. And in that moment, Conner thought about all the hardships Grace had experienced through the tragedies in her family.

"Your family has had a rough go of it."

She gave him a level gaze, then glanced down at the manila folder she had pulled out of her tote. She opened it on the table. A yellowed newspaper clipping fluttered with the motion. "I went into the basement of the library to read the articles that were written about my mother's murder." If he hadn't been watching her closely, he might have missed the small shudder that shook her thin frame.

Conner sat down on the bench across from her, resting his back against the table. Twisting, he put his elbow on the table. He dragged the top folder toward him. "So, it's official, you're going to write an article about your mother's murder?"

The burden weighing on him since Jason had died had lifted a fraction. But another part of him felt guilty. Had he added to Grace's burden while trying to ease his?

She smoothed her hand across a yellowed article, avoiding his face. "I'm *still* looking into the circumstances surrounding Jason Klein's death."

He ran his hand over the back of his neck. "Listen, you've had a rough day. I'll follow up and see if the deputies found anything in the basement. See if there's any video surveillance. Determine who did this."

She absentmindedly ran the tip of her finger across her lower lip. "I was thinking…" She opened up each of the manila folders and spread the articles out, and he studied the headlines in big black letters:

Amish Woman Murdered.

He scanned down to another.

No Suspect in Murder.

"See how big this headline is? The day after my mom died." He tracked her pink nail across several headlines, the font getting smaller, the articles getting shorter. "This is how it always goes. Big stories, big headlines, until the leads dry up and the story becomes an afterthought. The victim becomes an afterthought in everyone's mind except those they left behind."

He waited, sensing she wasn't done.

"That's why I do what I do. Well, partially…

I don't want people who can't speak for themselves to be forgotten."

"The Quail Hollow Sheriff's Department did everything they could to find your mother's murderer."

Grace closed the manila folder, articles poking out from the bottom and sides. The librarian in the purple dress would probably burst a blood vessel if she knew Grace had smuggled out the articles. "My intention isn't to malign the sheriff's department. Not at all. What if a fresh pair of eyes…"

Conner couldn't decide why he felt conflicted, when this was exactly what he had hoped she'd do when he set up the meeting between her and his father.

"I know I was the one who suggested this story, but do you really think it's a good idea?"

"Because of today? We don't know who knocked over the shelves. Maybe it had nothing to do with my mom. No one knows what I was researching. It could have been someone trying to scare me away from the other story. The story even you don't want me to investigate." She threaded her fingers and placed them in front of her on the table, on top of the manila folder.

Frustration weighed on him. "Whether it's digging into your mom's death or Jason's death, someone wants to stop you."

"Including you."

His intention had been to protect his family. Now, he had a growing need to protect her. "I don't want you to get hurt."

Grace looked up slowly. "I appreciate the concern, but I'm done talking about this for now. I'm really tired."

"Okay." He started to leave, then turned back. "Lock up when I go, and activate the alarm."

She stood and followed him to the door. Conner left and waited until he heard the dead bolt snap into place. Without turning around, he lifted his hand to wave. Despite her bravado, he suspected his words had hit their intended mark. If he was unsuccessful in deterring her from her research—whether it be about Jason or her mother—he feared someone else would succeed.

FIVE

Studying the oranges and reds of the flames visible through the slats on the wood-burning stove door did little to ease Grace's nerves. Resting her feet on the hearth, she tried to turn off all the thoughts crowding in on her. Since her sister had wanted guests to experience a somewhat authentic Amish home and the Amish didn't watch TV, Grace didn't have the luxury of zoning out in front of one. Conner's crack about the fridge came to mind. Her sister could run a bed & breakfast without a TV, but a fridge, not so much. Or at least without experiencing a lot of hassle.

In the short time since she had met Conner when he answered the call of the hit-and-run at the gas station, she had grown to like the man and his sense of humor, but she didn't like his message very much. He was beginning to make her paranoid. She couldn't do her job if she was afraid. When she was on her own, she was very good at dismissing red flags, and she hadn't been any worse for it.

After the night in the closet when her former brother-in-law terrorized her big sister, Grace vowed she'd never allow anyone to make her afraid. Not if she could help it.

Grace turned toward the window at the front of the house. While she was lost in thought, the sun had set, leaving the landscape beyond the front window black.

Anyone could be out there.

She tended to have that feeling a lot since she had been left alone to care for the bed & breakfast. She suspected it had more to do with her isolation out here in the country, in the dead of winter, than with anything nefarious.

At least, she prayed that was the case.

Pushing to her feet, she wandered to the window and stared out. She had to search past her reflection to see the white blanket of snow, only broken up by tire tracks, footprints and then the main road. Sighing heavily, she reached up for the white roller shade and had to struggle with it to pull it down. Her phone chimed next to the rocker, making her jump.

She laughed at herself—apparently she didn't need anyone to make her afraid. Her imagination was doing a perfectly good job of that.

Grace debated ignoring the phone, then decided against it. Maybe it was her editor. She should probably give him an update. He'd been salivating over the recent turn of events and how her Amish story would generate lots of clicks on their website.

"Amish is hot," he kept saying.

That was the part of the business she didn't like; however, if she wanted to write full-time, she realized her stories needed to generate revenue for the online news site. An Amish story of any magnitude would generate lots of clicks.

Pushing that thought aside, she picked up her phone. Surprise rippled through her. Her sister's radiant face stared up at her from the display, a photo taken at her wedding last spring. Smiling, Grace swiped her finger to answer. "Aren't you supposed to be on your honeymoon?" A honeymoon they had to delay until after the bed & breakfast's busy season.

"Ha! Can't a big sister check in on her little sister?" Heather said, sounding far more relaxed than when she and Zach had gone racing out the door with all their luggage in tow, afraid they were going to miss their flight out of Buffalo because of the weather. But they'd made it and were now on a three-week cruise somewhere in the southern hemisphere.

"Why do I feel like you're checking in on your B&B and not your little sister?" Grace settled back into the rocker and put her feet on the hearth.

"Can't I do both?" Heather laughed, and Grace thought she heard Zach saying something in the background. Grace was grateful her sister had finally found a good guy. A *really* good guy.

"All is well here." Grace didn't want to worry her sister. Hopefully she'd have the car repaired before she got back home. No harm, no foul. Besides, when Heather and Zach left town, Grace was mostly on the mend. They had no idea she was going to be using her recovery-slash-house-sit-the-B&B downtime to write a story about an underage party *and* investigate their murdered mother's cold case.

No rest for the weary.

"You're not bored? I thought maybe you'd be bored by now. There's not much to do compared to living in the city, and the cell reception can be spotty sometimes."

Grace smiled to herself, feeling a bit deceitful. "No, I'm fine." *I'm investigating two stories, and someone smashed your car and tried to crush me under library shelving. Beyond that...* "How's your trip going?"

As Heather told Grace about their ports of call and her sunburn, Grace thought she heard something at the back door. A soft scratching that made her freeze mid-rock in the rocking chair, straining to hear over her sister's update. With the phone pressed to her ear, she slid out of the rocker, crept toward the window over the seating area and tried to see who might be at the back door. Her view was obstructed.

Scratch-scratch-scratch.

Grace moved away from the windows and crept to the mudroom, the steady beat of her heart growing louder in her ears.

"Heather, is there a reason I'm hearing a scratching at the back door?" Grace laughed. Her nerves made it sound like an awkward squeak.

"Oh, that must be Boots."

Grace's shoulders relaxed. She couldn't imagine any ax murderer named Boots. "Is Boots a cat?"

"Of course." Her sister laughed.

"How come I've never met Boots before? I've been here for weeks."

"She's a stray. I thought she was gone for good. Haven't seen her in months. Thought maybe she had found her way back home. Oh, let her in. She must be freezing out there."

Really? Grace kept her thoughts to herself. Her mobile lifestyle meant she was used to caring for herself. Not stray animals.

"Okay..." Tucking the cell phone awkwardly between her ear and shoulder, she turned off the alarm and worked the lock on the back door. She opened the door a fraction, not quite sure what to expect, and a black cat with white paws slipped in and scampered over to the wood-burning stove and curled up on a pillow on the floor near the hearth that Grace hadn't noticed before. She turned the lock and followed Boots into the sitting room.

"She seems pretty comfortable." The cat licked her paws, effectively ignoring Grace.

"There's some cat food in the bottom cabinet by the oven in the kitchen. Boots will usually stay for the night and then want out in the morning. Poor thing was probably frozen out there. Oh, you're allergic. Maybe—"

"No, no, it's okay. I'll make sure she stays out of my bedroom. I'll be fine." Grace studied the cat, seemingly none the worse for wear. "I don't know how this kitty survived outside. It's freezing." A gust of wind beat against the side of the house, emphasizing her point.

"Your blood has thinned." Heather laughed. "After this trip, my blood might have thinned, too. The weather has been gorgeous."

"I'm glad to hear it. You deserve happiness."

"Thanks." After a pause, Heather added, "Is everything okay there? You sound a little subdued."

"Yeah," Grace said before quickly changing the subject. "You're sure Boots can stay for the night?" She crouched down and ran her hand across the cat's soft wet fur. "Dad would have never let us have an animal in the house."

"That was from his Amish days. Animals live in the barn." Heather cleared her throat. "It's hard not to think about Mom and Dad while you're at Mammy's old house, isn't it?"

"Yeah." Grace sat back down. *Even harder not to think of Mom when I've been researching her death.*

"I've gotten used to it after time. Mammy's home feels like my home now."

Grace traced the wood grain on the arm of the rocker. "Do you remember Mom?"

"Yes. Most of my memories seem dreamlike. You were three years younger."

"And Rose was just a baby," Grace said, staring at the flames in the stove. "She probably has no recollection of mom."

Heather's voice grew quiet. "Are you sure you're okay?"

"Oh, listen to me." She sat up a little straighter, feeling guilty for bringing up their dead mother while her sister was on her honeymoon. "Did I mention Rose sent me a nice fruit basket to wish me well on my recovery? She was always the thoughtful sister." She forced a cheery laugh.

"Who took care of you while you were recovering?" Heather said in mock disbelief. "Rose probably had someone in her office send it."

Grace smiled. It was a relief to both of them to know the youngest of the Miller sisters was doing well despite the tragedy that had befallen them as young children.

Grace stifled a yawn. "Sorry. I'm tired."

"Go curl up in bed with a good book. There's a library in the corner of the sitting room."

Grace had noticed the books. Maybe she would.

"Sounds nice. I might do that. Go enjoy your trip. Don't worry about things here. I've got it under control."

Zach yelled, "Hi, Grace!" in the background.

"Tell him to take care of you."

"I will." Her heart warmed at the smile she detected in her big sister's voice. Heather's happiness had been a long time coming.

On his way home, Conner swung by the grocery store to pick up a late dinner. Despite common misconceptions of bachelors living on takeout and cold cereal, Conner preferred to make a healthy dinner at home. The cooking relaxed him, and the food tasted better.

The automatic doors of the grocery store whooshed open, and a rush of hot air blasted him in the face as he grabbed a shopping basket. He would have offered to bring dinner over to Grace if he hadn't sensed she wanted time alone.

He reminded himself that she had a solid lock on the door and an alarm system.

Deciding that had to be good enough, he wandered through the produce section. He picked up a head of lettuce and inspected it.

"Exciting dinner plans?"

Conner turned to see Kevin Schrock, his father's former undersheriff, leaning one arm on the handle of an empty shopping cart and staring intently at him. Kevin and his father had worked together for years, and both bore the burden of never solving the only murder in Quail Hollow during their tenure.

"The life of a bachelor." Conner tossed the head of lettuce into his basket. He figured Kevin didn't really care what he was doing for dinner; he was merely looking for an opening to talk to him about something else.

"Don't I know it." Kevin sighed. A crooked smile hooked the side of his mouth. "But a young, good-looking guy like you shouldn't be a bachelor forever. Or at least you could get some pretty girl to offer to cook for you."

Conner pressed his lips together and shrugged. This wasn't exactly the type of conversation he cared to have.

"How's Grace Miller?" And there it was, the subject Kevin was angling to talk about.

Conner jerked his head back, unsure if Kevin knew about the incident in the basement library, or if he was simply making idle conversation regarding the new woman in town, who happened to be the daughter of the murdered Amish woman.

Conner decided to broach the subject directly. "You heard about the library?"

"Yes, a couple deputies were at the diner. Is Grace okay?"

"She's fine. She escaped without injury." Conner forced an even tone to his voice, trying not to think about how seriously Grace could have been injured.

"Do you know what happened?" It wasn't unusual for retired law enforcement officers to insert themselves into the thick of an active investigation, especially in a small town. Conner supposed it was more exciting than watching *The Price is Right* or whatever Kevin did in his spare time.

"We're still trying to figure that out."

"Do you think it has to do with the incident at the gas station? Because she's investigating Jason's death?" Kevin peppered him with questions, not taking a breath to wait for the answers. "What's in the library basement?" The retired officer straightened and ran his hand along the handle of the shopping cart. "Must be her mom's case, right? She was looking for those old articles your dad was telling her about?"

"We're still trying to figure that out, too." Conner took a few steps to his right and selected a cucumber for his salad.

"You need to be careful." Kevin pushed his cart closer to him, unwilling to take the subtle clues that Conner wanted to get his dinner and go home.

Conner tossed the cucumber into his basket and angled his head to give Kevin a curious look.

"Grace is a pretty girl. It's easy to look into those brown eyes and forget she's a reporter."

Conner bit back his annoyance. "I'm not really sure what you're getting at."

"Your dad told you how that reporter interfered during Sarah Miller's murder investigation."

"That was a long time ago."

"You're young. You're optimistic. Personally, I wouldn't trust Grace. If she finds something on Jason's accident and it comes out that you should have uncovered it first and missed it due to blind loyalty to family…" Kevin grimaced, suggesting loyalty to a fault would be a very bad thing indeed.

Anger simmered below the surface. Conner glanced around to make sure no one was listening. "I'm not covering up anything. Jason's mom has been through enough. She doesn't need more news coverage on her son's death." He blinked away the image of Jason's bloody face from where it had impacted the steering wheel.

Kevin held up his hands and backed away from his cart. "Easy, man. I know, I know. Remember, Sheriff Flatt's retiring next year. If you have any hopes of running for sheriff, you don't want any stink attached to your name."

"Listen, I don't go about doing my job wondering what's in it for me. I do my job the best I can." Conner glanced around. An older woman gave him a curious look and continued past. He had raised his voice louder than he'd intended.

"You're great at your job. It's just—" Kevin shrugged "—your dad's worried about you. He knows firsthand what it's like to be burned by a reporter. I'm trying to help. Your dad won't say anything himself."

His father hadn't mentioned anything to him, but that wouldn't be unlike his old man. He was forever trying to protect his son—the best he knew how—from everything from the blow of losing his mom to his day-to-day frustrations. Instead of easing Conner's mind, the secrecy only served to make him worry more. What else was his father hiding in an effort to protect his son?

Conner lifted his shopping basket as if to say, "Well, I gotta go," and forced a smile. "Don't worry about me or my career. I've got it handled."

"That's what your father used to say, until the unsolved murder and the relentless bad press made him realize he'd never be reelected."

Conner shook his head in confusion and immediately realized his mistake.

"You didn't know that, did you? You thought he rode off into retirement." Kevin shook his head with a smug expression on his face. "Your father had no intentions of retiring until that reporter ruined his career."

"That was a long time ago, Kevin."

The older man tipped his head. "Time doesn't heal all wounds."

An unfamiliar sound broke through Grace's restless sleep. She rolled over and tried to get comfortable before she heard it again. She froze and held her breath, straining to listen, to understand what had woken her up.

Since she had come here a few weeks back to recover from her appendectomy, she had grown accustomed to the sounds of the bed & breakfast, even in the dead of night. The tree branches scraping against the side of the house on the windiest of nights, the battery-operated clock ticking away the longest stretch of the night and the occasional drip from the faucet when she forgot to turn the handle just a little bit tighter to the right.

But this was something different.

Scratch-scratch-scratch.

There it was again. Her sleepy mind finally registered, and relief flooded her system. Boots! The cat she had let in. She must have come upstairs looking for her in the middle of the night.

Thankful that it wasn't some intruder creepily dragging a nail across her closed—and thankfully locked—bedroom door, she pushed back the covers and climbed out of bed. The hardwood floor was cold on her bare feet. She slid on her slippers and shuffled to the door. She didn't want to let Boots into the room where she slept because she was mildly allergic. She could deal with the cat taking refuge in the main living quarters of the bed & breakfast. That shouldn't aggravate her eyes too much.

The lock snapped when she twisted the knob, the sound echoing in the quiet house. She opened the door a crack. Boots darted into the room and disappeared under the bed. Narrowing her gaze at the shadows in the hallway, Grace wondered what had spooked the cat.

Instinctively, she leaned out and glanced down the stairs, unable to make out much in the black of night. Was someone down there? No, she wouldn't let her imagination get the best of her, despite the fluttery whisper of dread upsetting her stomach.

She wandered over to the bed and got down on her knees. Groaning, she lay flat on her belly on the hardwood floor. She was ready to be done with the post-surgery aches and pains. "Come on, scaredy-cat, you can stay warm and cozy downstairs. You can't sleep under my bed."

In the blackness, Grace couldn't make out any discernible shapes under the bed skirt. She pushed up on all fours and reached to pick up her cell phone from the bedside table. Turning on the flashlight app, she shined it under the bed. Cat eyes glowed back at her, taunting her. With one hand, she reached out and, remarkably, Boots moved toward her.

For her reward, Grace sat cross-legged, rested her back against the bed and petted the cat, itchy eyes or not. After a few minutes, Grace got to her feet with the cat in her arms. She set the phone down on the nightstand. "Let's take you downstairs to your cozy bed, okay? You'll be nice and warm next to the stove." Grace laughed at herself. She wondered if someday, after living alone for years, she'd become the crazy cat lady who had full-on conversations with cats. "Don't start talking back," she muttered, running her hand over the cat's head.

Grace's slippers made a soft flip-flop sound as she crossed her bedroom to the hallway and made her way down the darkened stairs. She skimmed the cold railing with her free hand. When she reached the bottom stair, she put the wriggling cat down on the floor.

Boots shot across the room and darted behind Heather's rolltop desk. *What in the world?* Goosebumps blanketed Grace's cool skin, which made her realize it was freezing down here. Had the wood-burning stove gone out?

Then something fluttered at the corner of her eye, followed by a loud clack. The roller shade beat against the window frame. Holding her breath, she took a step closer, and terror sent a wave of prickles across her scalp. Behind the askew shade, the window yawned wide.

Frozen with indecision for the briefest of moments, Grace weighed her options. With a confidence she didn't feel, she ran to the window, reached behind the shade, and slammed it down, twisting the lock at the top.

Why hadn't the alarm gone off? She raced to the panel and noticed the light was green. It wasn't activated. Had she been too distracted when talking to her sister to forget to reset it after she let Boots in?

She strained her brain to remember. She couldn't.

What if the intruder was still inside? She glanced toward the shadows where Boots had disappeared. The cat would be fine. She, on the other hand, was exposed.

She ran to the staircase, taking them two at a time, and reached her room. She slammed the door and locked it, then raced to her bedside table and turned on the light, casting away all the spooky shadows.

She swiped her cell phone from her bedside table. Clutching it to her chest, she kicked off her slippers—they'd slow her down if she had to run—and crept to her bathroom. She reached around the corner and flipped on the light. With her jagged breath in her ears, she moved forward and snatched back the shower curtain, then heaved a sigh.

Empty.

She pressed her cold hand to her neck. She was alone. At least up here.

For now.

For all her bravado, when push came to shove, she hated being afraid. Being unsure. Being vulnerable.

Someone had opened the window downstairs, and it wasn't the cat.

Grace slammed the bathroom door and locked it. With her back pressed against the door, she dialed Conner's number.

Dear Lord, help him get here in time.

SIX

"I'm pulling up the driveway now," Conner spoke to Grace on the phone, his words clipped. He canvassed the desolate landscape around the bed & breakfast. "Nothing visible out here. Everything okay on your end?"

He couldn't figure out why the alarm system hadn't gone off.

"Still safely locked in my bathroom." He didn't miss the trace of humor in her tone. It was a pleasant shift from the frantic call that had awoken him out of a sound sleep.

"I'm going to walk the perimeter." He climbed out of his truck and cringed when the cold air hit his exposed neck. "I'll see what's going on. Come downstairs in five minutes and open the back door." He didn't want to be distracted with the phone if someone was still out here.

When she didn't answer immediately, he added, "Okay?"

"Yes, thanks." The strain in her voice had been

replaced by relief. For someone who claimed she didn't need anyone, it surprised him.

Conner slid the phone into the pocket of his bulky coat and lifted his flashlight. Out in the country on a cloudy night, it was dark like the bottom of a well. The beam of the flashlight bounced off the white snow. Footsteps dotted the driveway and the pathways to the house. He directed the light toward the barn and the other outbuildings. Footsteps led out to both. Nothing out of the ordinary, considering the horses had to be cared for by a young Amish man. According to Grace, he also did a few odd jobs around the bed & breakfast.

Conner walked toward the house, the beam from his flashlight leading the way. Grace had said a window in the sitting room had been opened. He made a wide berth around the house in an attempt to preserve evidence. The snow underneath the corner window had definitely been trampled. He slid out his phone, took off his gloves, and took a few snapshots of the boot prints. From first glance, the prints looked like they could be from any number of boots worn by half the men he knew, including him. The images would have to be enlarged and studied more closely.

The forecast was calling for more snow. Snow that would obscure the prints in no time at all.

He slid his phone back into his pocket and

blew on his fisted hands to warm them up. On nights like this, he wondered why his dad hadn't retired to Florida by now. That was in Conner's twenty-year plan. Become sheriff. Retire. Move to Florida.

Conner stomped the snow from his feet on the back porch. "Come on, Grace." He quietly rapped on the door to avoid startling her. Just then, he heard her undoing the lock.

She pulled open the door, her hair mussed from sleep. She had pulled a fleece jacket over her pajamas.

"Are you okay?" Conner stepped into the small entryway.

"I guess I'm a trouble magnet."

Conner held up his hand. "Stay here. Let me check the house."

Grace's eyes flared wide. "You think he's still here?"

"Can't be too sure. Hold up." Conner did a quick canvass of the house, including the upstairs rooms that were often rented out to tourists during the warmer months.

When he came downstairs, he found Grace walking around the kitchen table, picking up the newspaper articles off the floor. Her long hair fell in a curtain, hiding her face. When she straightened, she tucked her hair behind her ear. She placed an article inside the manila folder. "I'm not sure if all the articles are still here."

She flattened the paper with her hand. "Maybe this is what someone was looking for. It seems the wind from the open window blew them off the table." She bent over and picked up another one. "I wouldn't be able to tell you what's here or what's not. I haven't had time to study all of them."

A small piece of paper was tucked under the leg of the table. He leaned over and picked it up. The paper felt brittle. It was dated six months after Sarah Miller's murder. The first line read: *Local Amish family has yet to return after mother's murder.*

"Here's one more."

Grace took the piece of paper, glanced at it briefly, then tucked it into the folder with the rest she had gathered. Her hip bumped the table, and the screen on her open laptop flickered to life. A photo of a smiling Grace beamed up at him from the screen. He caught sight of the title on the page: *Researching a Mother's Murder.*

His eyes met Grace's and she frowned. "My editor thinks this will go viral."

He furrowed his brow. "What do you think?"

Grace slowly sat down on the picnic-style bench and leaned back on the table. She threaded her hand through her hair and pressed her elbows together. "I haven't had a chance to think. When I arrived in Quail Hollow, I was sick as a dog. For the first few weeks, I was laid up in bed recovering from complications from my surgery. Once I was on the mend, I started to investigate Jason's accident, then my mom's murder, and—" she started to giggle and couldn't seem to stop "—it's been one thing after another."

She looked up and wiped the tears with the back of her knuckle. "Someone obviously doesn't want me to investigate something." She shrugged and took a calming breath to quell her giggle fit, the kind that struck when nothing was funny and you weren't supposed to laugh. "But what don't they want me to investigate? Jason's accident? Or my mother's murder?"

Conner sat on the bench next to Grace and nudged her shoulder. "We'll figure this out."

With a look of surprise glowing in her eyes, she opened her mouth to protest when he picked up her laptop from the table. "Nice photo."

"They caught me on a good hair day." She reached for the laptop.

"Wait. Can I read this?"

Her cynical expression said, "I don't know why you'd want to."

Conner skimmed through both the posts Grace had written and the teasers her editor had posted. It had specific details on her location as well as hints regarding her investigation. He tapped the screen and it flickered. "This right here makes you a sitting duck. This provides all the information someone needs if they want to hurt you."

* * *

Heat crawled up Grace's cheeks. She resented being treated like a teenager who had shared too much personal information on the internet. This was her job. Her job meant being visible online.

But had she foolishly put herself in jeopardy?

Normally when she was covering a story, she was staying in secure hotels, or she had long moved on to another town—another story—before her editor posted her work. Her extended stay in Quail Hollow and covering a story with a personal slant had been a game changer. Anyone with evil intent could know who she was and where she'd most likely be staying.

Annoyed and feeling more than foolish that she hadn't realized the risk, Grace leaned over and snapped the laptop closed. She took it from Conner's lap and placed it on the table a bit more roughly than she had intended.

"Most stories I write, I'm an anonymous reporter. I'm often done with the story and on to the next location before any information is posted online. People don't know where I'm staying." She pointed at the closed laptop for emphasis like Conner had. "My editor has insisted I post blogs until the bigger story is complete. I never felt like my safety was at risk." She pressed her palm to her neck and relished her cool fingers on her hot skin. "It's not like I can pick up and leave. I promised my sister I'd keep an eye on the bed & breakfast. It's the least I can do for her after all she's done for me."

"When will Heather and Zach be back?"

"The end of next week."

"You can't stay out here by yourself."

Instinctively, she bristled at his command. "I'll make sure I set the alarm this time." She dropped her hand and dipped her chin. "I must have forgotten to reset the alarm when I let Boots in." The green light glowing on the alarm display on the wall mocked her. "I don't know how I forgot. I needed to make sure Boots didn't go upstairs. I'm allergic. I mean, I'm okay, as long as cats don't roll around in my sheets." She smiled sheepishly, aware that she was talking too much.

As if sensing she had been called, Boots scooted out from wherever she had been hiding in all the commotion and brushed up against Grace's leg. If she wasn't worried about her eyes itching all day, she would pick up the cat and cuddle her. It wasn't Boots's fault that Grace had recklessly failed to reset the alarm. "I should have been more careful. I will be from now on."

Conner stood, planted his palms on the table and stared out over the yard. Grace turned to see whatever had captured his attention. Streaks of purple and pink stretched across the sky behind the barn. Today was going to be a very long day.

He pushed off the table and crossed his arms, ready to press his point. "I can't let you stay here alone."

Let her?

"I said I'd set the alarm. I won't forget again." She gritted her teeth to avoid saying something she knew she'd regret.

"Okay, you set the alarm," he said, his tone suggesting he was about to point out all the holes in her simple plan. "What do you do once someone breaks in again? The alarm's going off, blaring in the basement. You're out here alone. How long do you think it will take my department to respond? Do you know how many false alarms we get each day?"

"I'll call 9-1-1. Let them know it is an emergency," she bit out, frustrated that they even needed to have this conversation.

"Who knows what could happen while you're waiting for help?"

Grace fisted her hands. "I don't know. I'll get a gun!" she quickly added, determined not to be forced out of the bed & breakfast, despite her fear of guns. She had covered far too many stories where a gun in the wrong hands had changed someone's life with the pull of a trigger.

Conner closed the distance between them and glared down at her, using his height to intimidate her. "Do you know how to use a gun?"

"I can learn," she said with a trace of indignation, standing her ground.

"What do you do in the meantime?" Conner had a question for everything.

"I said I'd set the alarm."

"It seems we're talking in circles."

A quiet knock sounded on the door. Grace was relieved for the distraction and took a step toward it.

"Let me get it." Conner brushed past her and opened the door. A part of her wanted to bump him out of the way and tell him that it was *her* door. Someone had come to see *her*. A cooler head prevailed and she didn't act on her childish instincts, despite feeling humiliated.

Instead, she forced a cheery smile at the young Amish man standing at the door.

"Morning, Eli." Then, noticing the concerned look on his face, she added, "Is everything okay?" Perhaps he had seen something—or someone—in the barn.

"Um…" Eli palmed the top of his black knit winter hat. Blunt bangs jutted out, skimming the tops of his eyebrows. "Everything's okay. It's just…" His nose twitched. "Maybe…"

Grace slipped in front of Conner, thinking perhaps Eli was reluctant to talk to someone in law enforcement. Eli took a step backward, and Grace hoped she wouldn't have to follow him out into the snow. Clutching her collar closed, she blinked against the blowing snow. How did he work in these conditions? "Wait, Eli. Please come in. Conner is leaving if you'd prefer to talk in private."

"Um…" Something like regret, or maybe doubt, flashed across the man's face.

Curiosity had made Grace's nerve endings buzz, like when a story was about to break wide open.

"I'm not going anywhere," Conner muttered, standing directly behind her. Grace had to will herself not to nudge him with her elbow, fearing Eli would forget the whole thing and run off.

Eli flipped up his collar against the wind and tucked in his chin. Grace wished he'd come in the house already. "The horse needs to be fed." He mumbled a few words, then said, "I heard something."

"In the barn?" Conner's watchful gaze scanned the snow-covered field and stopped at the new barn.

"*Neh*, not in the barn."

"Come in." Grace pushed the door open wider, and Eli finally accepted her invitation. The Amish man didn't take off his hat or indicate that he had any intention of taking off his coat or coming in farther than the back mudroom. Conner must have also sensed the young man's apprehension, and he and Grace both waited for Eli to speak.

The worried young man studied the room, barely making eye contact. "I heard some guys talking at the hardware store yesterday." Eli bit his thumbnail, clearly more comfortable with the horses he tended than the people who owned them.

"Go on," Grace encouraged.

"They were laughing about the lady who got run down at the gas station."

Grace shot a look at Conner, who seemed more interested in watching Eli. Anticipation vibrated through her entire body.

"Do you know these guys?" Conner asked.

Eli shook his head. "*Neh.* I've seen them around, but I don't know them. The way they were talking, it made me wonder if they knew what happened to Miss Heather's car at the gas station."

"What else did you hear?" asked Grace.

"They said they heard the truck that hit you was parked behind Katy Weaver's barn."

"Katy? The young Amish woman who was hurt in the accident after the drinking party?" Grace's heart raced in her ears.

"*Yah*, that's why I had to come forward. Katy's a *gut* friend of my sister's. Their family has been through a lot." Eli turned to Conner. "Maybe you can move the truck to spare the family finding it."

"Yes, absolutely," Conner said. "Are there any other males living in the Weaver household?"

Grace wondered if Conner's thoughts were heading down the same path as hers. Had someone in Katy's house been driving the truck? It all seemed a bit too coincidental.

"*Yah*, Katy's *dat* and her brother." Eli fisted and unfisted his gloved hands, before he stuffed them under his armpits and rocked up on the balls of his heavy work boots. "Levi."

A blanket of goosebumps raced across her arms, and her mouth grew dry.

Eli reached for the door handle, having said what he came to say. "I better feed the horses and get back home to my chores."

"Wait," Conner said, while Grace tried to process what she had heard. A part of her was ashamed that her brain automatically turned to crafting the first few lines of the post that would have her readers gasping: *Truck that narrowly missed me found behind the barn of the Amish girl fighting for her life after a separate accident.*

She stopped mentally composing her prose and said a quiet prayer that Katy's brother had nothing to do with the incident at the fuel pumps. They'd seemed like a close-knit family when she briefly met them, before they told her they wanted their privacy.

Grace ran a hand over her forehead. What purpose would it serve for Levi to hurt her? What was Grace missing about the night of the accident?

She snapped out of her wandering thoughts. "Would you recognize these guys from the hardware store if you saw them again?" she asked Eli.

"*Yah*, well, the way they were talking, it sounded like they were repeating what they had heard. Probably at school." He shrugged, the edges of his collar brushing against his cheeks. "I don't want to get into trouble. With everything else that's going on, I don't want to bring any shame to my family or my Amish neighbors." The Amish might not watch TV, but they had been well aware of the news reports that painted their community in an unflattering light.

"Thanks, Eli. You won't get into trouble," Grace said reassuringly.

The amount of information Grace gleaned because people failed to keep their mouths shut never ceased to amaze her. Far more criminals would get away with things if they didn't feel the need to boast, like whoever had bragged about parking the truck on the Weavers' property.

"I need to do my chores here and then get back home."

Conner nodded. "I appreciate your coming forward. I can't imagine it was easy."

"I had to. I saw you in the kitchen through the window. I hardly slept last night." Eli scratched his forehead under his bangs. "The outside world is evil." Then his eyes flared wide, realizing he may have offended them. "I hope they find whoever tried to hurt you." He flicked a look in her direction, then ducked his head and opened the door. Cold air filled the small space.

"Thank you, Eli," Grace quickly added, to reassure him. "You did the right thing." He took large steps across the deep snow to the barn. She closed the door and leaned against the cool wood, meeting Conner's gaze. "We have to go to the Weavers' house now. See if the truck is really there."

SEVEN

"Eli said the Weavers live three houses from the intersection of County and Pautler. It should be…" Grace tugged on her seat belt and leaned forward, straining to see past the wipers whooshing on high to keep up with the falling snow. Were they about to find out who rammed her car?

What if it's Katy's brother? The family would be devastated all over again.

"What are you going to say to Levi?" Grace asked, trying to focus on something productive and not all the what-ifs.

"Let's approach him and see what he knows about the truck." Conner adjusted the wipers to a lower speed.

"How likely is it that Levi's parents would allow him to store a truck at their home, even if it is his running-around years?" The irony that Grace had been born to Amish parents and had to ask Conner these questions wasn't lost on her.

Keeping his narrowed gaze on the disappearing road markers ahead, Conner said, "Some teens do drive cars, but their parents would hardly condone it by allowing them to keep the vehicle on their property. More often than not, if an abandoned vehicle is reported, it belongs to a young Amish man who has nowhere to park it but is eager to see what all the fuss is about. However, once they're baptized into the Amish faith, they have to give up cars and driving. It's a big decision for young adults to be baptized. In the end, most do choose to be baptized. It's what they know."

"That might explain why my dad knew how to drive when we left to live in Buffalo." She blinked the thought away, better left to explore on another day.

She pointed at a simple farmhouse with a long porch and no railings. "The Weaver house should be right here."

"Before we knock on the door," Conner said, "I want you to know I only agreed to bring you along because I didn't want you wandering over here alone."

She knew he didn't have to accommodate her. "I appreciate it. I'd really like to know who rammed my car—my sister's car—at the gas station."

"I need you to promise me you won't publish

online any information we uncover here today until *after* we have things wrapped up."

"What constitutes wrapped up?" An edge of annoyance seeped into her tone. Some cases were never wrapped up, and she wasn't going to wait forever.

"Sit on the information until I give you the okay."

She leaned back in her seat, feeling like she was being confined by more than a seat belt. She worked alone. She preferred it that way. "I won't compromise the investigation," she said, unable to keep the defensive tone from her voice.

Conner nodded in agreement. He had called the tip about the truck into the station, and the sheriff agreed that he could go to the Amish residence out of uniform in hopes they'd be more receptive to talk to him.

They parked in the Weavers' snow-covered driveway. A fresh footpath in the newly fallen snow connected the house to the barn. Even in the dead of winter, the animals needed to be cared for.

"Do you think Katy's parents saw the truck? Where did Eli say it was parked?" Grace wrapped her hand around the door release. "Behind the barn, right?"

"Yes, that's what he heard. And I doubt the Weavers know it's there otherwise they would have had it removed." Conner flipped up the collar on his coat, bracing for the cold. "Let me do the talking. See what's going on."

She opened her mouth to protest, and he cut her a sideways look. "Work with me, please."

Grace nodded. She decided she'd get more information if Conner was on her side. Up until now, the sheriff's department had blocked all her attempts at getting any information that wasn't already public knowledge.

"You ready?" he asked.

Grace wrapped her scarf around her neck and made sure her hat covered her ears. She'd never get used to this weather. "Ready."

They both climbed out of his truck. The snow made a squeaky, crunching noise under their hurried footsteps. Neither seemed willing to prolong this errand. Part of Grace hoped they found the truck—it would be a big lead—and another part of her prayed the Weaver family didn't have to face any more bad news.

"Before we upset the family, let's wander around behind the barn and see if we can find the truck. If there's nothing there, we can get out of here." Conner gently took her by the elbow.

He had read her mind. She had no interest in causing the family any more distress.

They moved past the well-worn path between the house and barn, through snowdrifts up to her knees. "Remind me why people live here?" she joked between chattering teeth.

A white cloud of vapor exhaled from his nose. He muttered something about taking up skiing.

When they reached the corner of the barn, they were met by a field of pristine snow. Grace fell back on the heels of her boots, and a clump of snow slipped into her boot. She tugged on the ends of her scarf, pulling it tighter. "There's nothing here." Grace wasn't sure what to feel beyond a growing eagerness to slip off her boots and warm her feet by the stove.

She sniffed. "Maybe Eli misunderstood what he overheard. We should talk to him again." She shoved her gloved hands into the pockets of her jacket. A snowflake landed on her eyelash and she blinked it away.

"There's another outbuilding across the field." Conner pointed to a dilapidated shed further back on the property.

Grace groaned. "The snow has to be two feet with drifts." She lifted one boot, then the other, already imagining her toes turning into ice chunks inside her boots—technically, her sister's boots. She hoped to never have a need for winter gear again.

"I'll go. Wait here or—" he handed her the keys "—inside the truck. Stay warm." Without waiting for an answer, Conner strode toward the building that had seen better days. It was the only other spot on the property where someone could hide a truck.

Disheartened, Grace turned to head toward Conner's truck, already envisioning the warm heat pumping from the vents. She didn't relish wet socks, but it'd be better than frozen toes. When she passed the barn, a young Amish man about Eli's age came out, a curious look on his clean-shaven face.

Levi Weaver.

Grace wasn't sure who was more surprised. A look of worry flashed in his eyes. Before he had a chance to speak, she said, "I'm sorry, I didn't mean to surprise you. You're Katy's brother." She had met him previously and he had chased her away. She hoped time had made him more receptive to talk to her.

"*Yah.*" The young man looked around, sensing that she wasn't alone. "Did something happen? My parents are inside. They were going to visit Katy today until the snow came."

"No, no…" She drew in a quick breath and measured her words. Her limbs instantly went heavy. He must have thought she'd come here with news of his sister's condition. She had tremendous empathy for the young man. She knew what it was like to have your family ripped apart by tragedy.

But what if he wasn't innocent?

Grace pointed toward the footsteps in the snow. Conner had disappeared behind the shed at this point. "Captain Gates is looking to see if a truck is parked behind the shed. Do you know anything about that?"

The young man fidgeted with the cuffs on his coat. *"Neh."* He lifted his gaze to his home. His family was inside. Everyone except his sister. What had made him so jittery all of a sudden?

"Several nights ago," she started, "I went to the gas station to talk to someone about the party that took place the night your sister was injured. I wanted to find out what happened. Someone rammed my car with a big truck." She took a step closer to him. His downcast eyes were hidden under his long bangs made straighter by his snug-fitting knit hat. Snowflakes landed and melted from the heat of his head.

"My sister has been in the hospital ever since her accident."

"How is she doing?" Grace asked, encouraged that he was opening up.

A sad smile curved his mouth as he continued to study the snow. Soon he'd get married and a long beard would cover his jaw. "The doctors are encouraged. She woke up last night."

"That's wonderful." Grace reached out to touch his arm in a show of support, then let it drop, deciding it might not be welcomed.

"They're not sure when she'll be able to come home."

"I'll keep her in my prayers."

Levi finally lifted his weary eyes to meet hers. Didn't he believe she'd pray for her?

"Had you gone out the night of your sister's accident?"

"*Yah*, I took my courting wagon to the singing." Grace imagined it was exactly as it sounded. He hadn't been with his sister because he had been bringing a girl home. His words dripped with regret. "My sister had dropped off her friends, two sisters who live not far from the accident. It was a very *gut* thing they weren't hurt, too." His voice grew soft.

"I'm so sorry." The pain etched in his features broke her heart.

A dark intensity suddenly lit his eyes. "You need to leave before my parents see you."

"Okay." Grace turned to see Conner plodding through the snow toward her. From this distance, she couldn't tell whether or not he had found anything. "Here's Captain Gates now. We'll leave. We don't mean to cause you any pain. If you want to talk in the future, I'm staying at the Quail Hollow Bed & Breakfast."

Breathing heavily, Conner reached the snow-packed clearing where Grace stood with Katy's brother. Clumps of snow had attached to his pants. He gave her a subtle nod, indicating that he had found the truck. Her adrenaline spiked and she wanted to ask Levi a million questions. Yet she was empathetic to the young man's vulnerability and held back. "Captain Gates, this is Katy's brother, Levi."

Conner stuck out his hand, and the Amish man glanced at it, clearly uncomfortable. Realizing he wasn't going to take it, Conner slipped his hand back into his pocket. "Son, do you know how the truck ended up behind the building back there?"

The young man's eyes widened. *"Neh."*

"Did you see it?"

He shook his head, crossed his arms and seemed to sink deep into the collar of his coat. "We don't have a reason to go back there. That's the old barn. It's falling apart. We have this new one right here."

"Levi, I know you've had a tough time of it. If you *do* know anything about the truck parked on your family's property, you need to tell me." A muscle twitched in Conner's jaw. "Maybe we can clear this up without getting your parents involved. They've been through enough."

Conner looked into the fearful eyes of the young Amish man. His sister was in a coma because of Jason, his cousin's son. The Amish only wanted to live peacefully, yet the outside world—Conner's world—was forever encroaching on their attempts at a peaceful existence.

"If you know something," Conner repeated, "you can talk to us."

"I've explained that to him," Grace said. "Right, Levi? You know you can confide in us."

Conner caught the grief-stricken expression on Levi's face before the Amish man bowed his head to hide the emotions playing across his features. Conner's mind flashed back to the photo his father had kept of Sarah Miller's three young daughters, taken surreptitiously a few days after their mother's murder. Conner had never seen such a quiet display of unbearable grief as he had in the portrait of the three motherless girls. Perhaps until today. Conner's father had claimed that photo motivated him to keep pursuing the case until time and lack of leads made it fruitless.

"How is your sister doing?" Conner asked.

"She's awake and doing better." He kicked the edge of the snow.

"That's good to hear." He hadn't realized how good until a sense of relief flooded him. "How do your parents get back and forth to Buffalo, to the hospital?"

"They hire a driver."

"The weather is supposed to clear up. Maybe I can drive your family to the hospital later."

Levi shook his head. "That's okay. I don't think my parents would want to take a ride from law enforcement. We like to stay separate."

"That's harder to do more and more." Conner tried to connect with the young man, who seemed to be standing on the edge of making a decision, one that would keep him among the Amish or one that would forever separate him from his family. Grace touched Conner's arm sympathetically and stepped away, allowing him to try to talk with the young man without her hovering.

"I found a truck behind the shed. Any idea how it got there? I'll keep it in confidence."

"I've been explaining..." The frustration was evident in Levi's tone. "After my sister's accident, the bishop spoke to us all at Sunday service. He said the youth of this community are making all the Amish look bad. If anyone is caught drinking or breaking the rules of the *Ordnung*, they will be punished." His lower lip quivered. "The Amish have never condoned this type of behavior, but now there is no tolerance."

"I thought the Amish were all about forgiveness." Conner watched the young man carefully.

"The leaders are frustrated. They feel like they've lost control." Levi ran a gloved hand under his nose. "I can't take that chance of bringing shame to my family."

Levi wasn't going to give him anything worth pressing for. Conner glanced down the driveway and saw the engine running on his truck. At least Grace was warm.

Conner shifted to brace himself against the wind and jammed his hands into his coat pocket. "I'm going to share something with you." He took a calming breath. "I'm Jason Klein's cousin, and my entire family feels horrible that your sister was hurt in the accident."

Levi cut a look toward Conner, then looked away.

"Jason's dad was killed last year while serving in the army. I was supposed to look out for the kid. I failed him."

Levi shifted from one foot to the other.

"And I failed your family." Conner fought to keep his voice from shaking. "I know you're cold." He glanced toward Levi's house. "I'm guessing you don't want to go inside to talk."

Levi shook his head. "My parents are in there." He ran a hand over his mouth.

"The sheriff's department is going to have to tow the truck off your parents' property, maybe after the snow melts." Conner hadn't thought that far ahead. "We can talk to your parents. I'll assure them someone else dumped it there and that you had nothing to do with it." Conner was pretty good at reading people, and he suspected Levi was innocent in all this.

Levi let out a long, frustrated breath. "I was at that party with the kid—your cousin—who crashed into my sister's wagon," he muttered, his words almost lost on a gust of wind.

"Did you hang out with him?" Conner's heart beat wildly in his ears. This was not at all what he had expected.

Levi stared at him for a long moment, his nose growing red from the relentless wind. He chipped away at the flattened snow with the tip of his black boot. "Some guys were arguing with him at the party. They were blaming Jason for getting them in trouble. Jason left the party pretty quick."

"Trouble? What kind of trouble?"

"I'm not really sure. They were making pig noises."

Like he's a squealer? A million thoughts pinged around Conner's brain.

"Do you know those kids?"

"Yeah, from around."

Conner didn't know if it mattered. Didn't know if it played into Jason's death. Just because a few guys had words at a party didn't mean anything, necessarily. Conner scrubbed a gloved hand across his face. He and Grace had built the frame and grouped like colors, yet the final puzzle pieces didn't quite fit.

The tips of his ears stung from the cold.

"Listen, I'm not sure a tow truck can access the back of your property. Not until spring." He pulled out a piece of paper from his pocket. "I have the registration number of the truck. The sheriff's department will be able to determine who owns it. If you'd like, I can talk to your parents. Tell them it was abandoned. This way you won't get in trouble with them or the leaders."

Levi glanced toward the house wearily. "I'll talk to them." He shuddered. It was far too cold to be standing out here talking. "You think that's the truck that tried to run over your friend?"

Conner tipped his head. "There's some back-end damage. Could be."

Levi nodded tightly.

"Everything will be okay." Conner turned to walk away when Levi started to say something.

Conner turned back.

"Jason and I were friends. We met last summer while working for Able."

His young cousin had dug post holes all summer long while working for a fence company. "You worked for Able Fencing, too?" Conner felt like he was getting more bits and pieces of information the longer he talked to Levi. It would be his job to put the information together.

Levi nodded, and all the color drained from his face. "*Yah*, Jason was a *gut* kid. He didn't drink or do drugs."

Conner froze, the new information jolting his system. "Are you sure?" It didn't make sense, anymore than the final report that speculated Jason had taken a handful of prescription drugs during what kids called pharming parties. Conner could hardly believe Jason would participate in such risky behavior. But blood results didn't lie.

"*Yah*, we were hanging out that night. He only

came to the party because a girl he liked was there. We had some hot chocolate, that's all. He told me he wasn't feeling well all of a sudden. When he was heading to the truck, some guys started yelling at him and chasing him. He tore out of the party right quick." Levi kicked the snow, and chunks shot in different directions. "One of the guys yelling at him was the mayor's son."

"Bradley Poissant? Are you sure? Jason and Brad have been friends since preschool."

"It was him. I've seen the kid around." That seemed to be the standard answer. Quail Hollow wasn't that big.

"But you don't know what they were arguing about?"

Levi slowly shook his head. "Look, I have to go in."

"All right then. Thanks for taking the time to talk to me." Conner walked back to his truck while Levi jogged toward his house.

Grace was tracking Levi's movements when Conner climbed back into the warmth of his truck. He was still processing the latest bit of news. Bradley and Jason had been arguing the night of Jason's fatal accident. Why hadn't Bradley told him? Perhaps guilt that their lifetime friendship had ended after a fight?

Conner tugged off his gloves and dragged a

hand through his hair, shaking off the snow. He grabbed his cell phone out of the drink holder in the console between them and punched in a few numbers. "I need to know who registered that vehicle." He gave the deputy the registration information and hung up.

"Is it the truck that crashed into me?" Grace asked.

"It has damage."

"If it walks like a duck, talks like a duck…" She smiled wearily. He stared back, still trying to figure out why Jason was arguing with his best friend the night he died.

Grace shifted in her seat. "What happened back there? You and Levi seemed to have a pretty intense conversation."

Conner stared straight ahead, watching the dizzying swirl of snow. "Levi told me that Jason didn't drink or do drugs." This matched what Jason had tried to tell him the night Conner broke up the bonfire. He loosened his collar. When pressed, didn't most kids claim they didn't drink?

"What? How is that possible?" Grace had read the reports. "Perhaps he had a low threshold."

"I don't know. Levi claimed he wasn't taking drugs or drinking alcohol that night. Levi said he left after saying he didn't feel well."

"What are you thinking?"

He shifted in his seat, avoiding her eyes. Was he taking a leap? "What if someone drugged him?"

"You mean, spiked his drink? He wasn't drinking."

"Levi said they had hot chocolate."

"Who would do that to him?"

Conner shook his head. None of this made sense. He'd been arguing with his best friend. No, none of this made sense. "I don't know."

His phone rang and he jumped. The dispatcher. "That vehicle is registered to a Paul Handler on Oak Grove."

"Thanks." He ended the call.

"You have a name?"

"Yeah."

Grace tapped the dash. "Let's go."

"I need to take you home."

"Aren't you going to take me with you? Keep me out of trouble?" She was hard to say no to.

"Yeah, I suppose you're right." Despite not wanting to put Grace in the center of his investigation, he preferred to keep an eye on her.

"Maybe I can ID him. I saw his profile at the gas station." Even Conner knew that was a stretch.

Before he lost his nerve and came to his senses, Conner jammed the gear into Drive. "Let's see about the owner of that truck."

EIGHT

Conner and Grace had almost reached the address of the truck owner when his cell phone buzzed. He glanced down and stifled a groan. The sheriff. His boss. He let it ring a few more times, debating if this phone call would somehow deter their little visit.

"You going to get that?" Grace asked, curiosity lighting her eyes.

Conner twisted his lips as if to say, "Maybe, maybe not." Who was he kidding? Of course he was going to get it, but he had to decide how he was going to handle it first. Letting out a long breath between tight lips, Conner grabbed the phone from his cup holder and swiped his thumb across the screen. "Sheriff." He forced a cheery tone that sounded stiff and insincere.

"How'd things go at the Weavers?" The men tended to dispense with formalities, getting right to the point.

"Fine."

"That's it? Fine? Care to elaborate? I hear you got a lead on the hit-and-run from the gas station."

"Yes, we did. I traced the owner. I'm at their address now."

"You're still in plain clothes, right?"

Conner rubbed his jaw with his palm. "Yeah." He was unable to hide the skepticism from his voice. His boss had given him the okay to stop by the Weavers' in plain clothes, hoping it would be less intimidating for the folks who didn't care to talk to law enforcement, even in the best of circumstances.

"Report for your shift, then track down the owner of the truck." The clock on the dash told him he was fifteen minutes past the start of his shift.

"I'm already here. I need to talk to the owner before word gets out. I want to catch him off guard. See what his excuse is." He thought back to the Amish man seeking him out this morning at the bed & breakfast. It was only a few hours ago, yet it felt like a lot longer, perhaps because now he had new information about his cousin. Information about him not feeling well prior to leaving the party. About not drinking. Conner shook his head, trying to clear it. He hadn't had time to process all the jumbled information and what it meant, if anything.

No matter how all this unfolded, at the end of the day, Jason would still be dead. The familiar fist of grief sat like a rock in his chest.

"See you in ten," the sheriff said, still pressing the issue that he report to the station immediately.

"I'm sitting in front of the residence now," he repeated to the sheriff, giving Grace an exasperated look. "Let me shake a few trees. See what falls out."

The sheriff's impatient sigh sounded over the line, and Conner imagined him leaning way back in his leather chair with one hand behind his head, his feet perched on the corner of the desk. "You got the reporter with you?"

Conner turned away from Grace, as if that would make a difference. "What's this about?" A sure way to act innocent: answering a question with another question.

"I hear you're getting chummy with her. Don't do anything stupid to jeopardize your career."

Gritting his teeth, Conner adjusted the vent on the dash to clear the frost from the windows. No, he didn't think he was getting "chummy" with the reporter. But he was limited in what he could say with her sitting inches away.

"Your silence speaks volumes." Conner imagined his boss's chair crashing forward, his feet slamming onto the floor and his face growing red with rage.

"Look, I have to go. I'll report back in after I talk to the truck's owner." Conner swiped the red button on his phone while the sheriff was still talking. It sounded like, "Who's the owner?" Conner would deal with the repercussions of hanging up on the sheriff later.

Grace casually gestured to his phone. "What was that all about?"

"Nothing."

She frowned, not exactly convinced.

"One problem at a time," Conner muttered, turning his focus on the situation at hand.

The Handlers' small white ranch house was ahead. His boss wasn't going to be happy with him for going against his request. It was a request, right? Not an order? He ignored the band of hesitation constricting his chest. Mentally, he was already calculating how much vacation he might be able to take if he needed to do some digging on his own. He had a sense the sheriff was about to put him on desk duty. And even if his boss did find the humor in his subordinate hanging up on him, Conner needed to be able to follow up on some things without the sheriff breathing down his neck.

There was no way Conner could give up exploring the path he was already on, because in the short time he had gotten to know Grace, he knew *she* wouldn't be easily deterred.

* * *

"I'm going with you," Grace said, hopping out of the truck before Conner even dared make the suggestion.

"And I'm doing the talking."

She twisted her lips in a wry expression. He'd accept that as agreement, but had his doubts even before they climbed the front steps of the Handlers' porch.

Conner lifted his hand to knock when the door flung open. Jenny Handler, a woman in her mid-forties, came up short, her purse swinging on the sleeve of her puffy winter jacket. "Oh." Surprise lit her eyes. Obviously, she had been on her way out and hadn't expected visitors to be standing on the other side of the door.

"Captain Gates." She tilted her head in recognition, and deep ridges lined her forehead. "Is something wrong?" She glanced over her shoulder, and her expression softened, perhaps after she had a chance to realize two things: her son was home and Conner was dressed in plain clothes, indicating he was unlikely to deliver bad news.

Maybe. Maybe not.

"Hi, Jenny. Is your husband around?" His name was on the truck's registration, after all, not hers.

Jenny leaned back on her heels and a cheerless smile slanted her lips. "You haven't heard?"

Conner frowned. "Clue me in."

"Paul took a job in Buffalo last summer."

"Ah, that's tough. Maybe the economy will pick up here soon."

She ran her hand down her fuzzy scarf. "Not sure it really matters." He didn't want to read more into that than he had to. Her marriage was none of his business. Right now, he needed to find out why her husband's truck was parked on the Weavers' property with damage consistent with a hit-and-run.

"What's going on?" Her gaze drifted to Grace. "Where's Paul's pickup?"

"That heap of junk? Out in his workshop, I guess." She paused a moment and stared at him. "What's going on?"

"We found a truck registered to your husband on the Weavers' property."

"The family of that poor Amish girl who was in that horrible accident? I don't understand." She loosened the scarf from around her neck and pulled off her knit cap. Wisps of blond hair stood straight up from the static. "Come in." She waved to them. "Charlie!" she hollered, clearly annoyed. "Get in here." She smoothed her hair and glanced expectantly toward a short hallway. "Charlie!" she hollered again. "Now!"

Then, turning toward her guests, "My son

has a late start to school because his first two classes are free." Conner smiled. At this exact moment, he wasn't worried if Charlie was truant; he wanted to know if he had used his father's truck.

Muffled grumbling preceded a door opening. A young kid appeared, pulling a sweatshirt over his bare chest. "What, Mom? What's wrong?" The teenager squinted at the three adults standing in the living room with the look of a person who had stepped out into the bright sun after an afternoon matinee.

"Hi, Charlie," Conner said. "I'm Captain Gates. This is Grace Miller. She was the woman nearly run down at the gas station the other night." Conner was watching the young man's expression carefully, but he took that exact moment to bend over and adjust his sock. Conner waited for him to straighten before continuing. "We found your father's truck."

Charlie's eyebrows scrunched up, and he shrugged. "Dad's truck?" He turned slowly, still seemingly struggling to come out of a dream state. "Isn't Dad's truck in his workshop out back?"

Conner was pretty good at reading people, and nothing about this kid screamed "liar." The kid was on edge, however. Maybe he was hiding something.

"Did you take out your dad's truck?" his

mother asked, frustration weighing heavily on her slumped shoulders. "Please don't tell me you took his truck out and crashed it. I'll never hear the end of it. You know how your father is."

"No way. I didn't, Mom."

The kid was afraid of his father and wouldn't borrow his truck, even if his dad had taken a job in Buffalo and hadn't bothered to come home to know the difference.

Charlie pushed back the hood of his sweatshirt and scrubbed his cropped hair. "I don't understand. Where did you find the truck?" He turned to his mom. "I thought Dad had the Chevy?"

"He does."

"Do you know Levi Weaver?" Conner asked.

"The Amish kid?" He shrugged. "Yeah, I've met him around." All the teenagers seemed to know all the other teens in town from "around."

"The truck was parked behind a run-down shed on their farm." Conner let the back of his hand brush Grace's, thankful she was allowing him to take the lead. She didn't make any indication that she recognized the kid as the driver of the truck that smashed into her. That would have been a long shot, anyway.

"How'd it get there?" Charlie's entire face scrunched up, as if he were trying to remember the formula to a complicated math problem.

"How many people knew the truck was parked in the workshop?" If someone knew Jenny's husband had left town, they could have taken the truck easily. Someone could borrow it without worrying about it being missed, for a while, anyway.

Charlie's eyes widened. If he had remembered something, he quickly tried to hide it by lifting his fist to his mouth and coughing.

"Did you remember something, Charlie?" Grace asked.

The young man turned to his mother with a hangdog expression. This was obviously a kid used to working his mom over to get his way.

"What is it, Charlie? Come on, spit it out." His mother unzipped her coat while speaking in a slow, methodical manner, as if she had grown weary of being a single parent to a teenage boy.

"It's nothing," he said through gritted teeth. Was he hoping his mother would "get it" without him saying whatever it was?

His mother took a step forward and turned around to stand next to her son. She put a hand on his back, clearly indicating she was on his side no matter what happened. "Charlie's a good kid. He has a scholarship to college this fall." She had the look of a woman who had already lost too much. "Please, he's on the right path. I don't think he'd do anything to screw that up." Conner wondered if this was wishful thinking on her part.

"A scholarship. That's great." Conner smiled

at the young man, wondering if perhaps Charlie had gotten in over his head on something and needed an ally to open up to. Conner had gone away to school thinking he wanted to escape his small-town roots, only to return and follow in his father's footsteps. "What college are you going to?"

"University at Buffalo." The young man stuffed his hands deep into the pockets of his jeans, probably the same pair he had dropped on the floor next to his bed the night before.

"Any chance you let one of your friends borrow your dad's truck?" Conner used his most reassuring tone.

When Charlie didn't answer, his mother glared at him. "You let one of your friends borrow the truck? What were you thinking?"

"No!" The exasperation in Charlie's voice might have been a bit over the top to be genuine.

"Who knew the truck was there?" Conner kept his tone even. The kid needed to feel like he was on his side.

Charlie leaned back on the arm of the over-stuffed couch. Apparently, he couldn't tell the truth with his mom standing next to him. "I had a few friends over last weekend. We were hanging out in the barn. That's where my dad has his workshop."

"What? Why would you hang out there? All your father's stuff..." A flicker of realization widened her eyes. "Aw, why, Charlie? You could lose your scholarship if they find out you're drinking."

"I don't think that could happen," Charlie said. "Besides, I *wasn't* drinking."

His mother looked like she was going to grind her teeth to nubs in an effort to keep quiet.

Charlie jerked one finger in her direction. "One beer. That's hardly anything."

Jenny put a hand over her mouth. "Charlie! Is it worth it?" She held out her open palm toward their visitors, indicating it obviously wasn't. "You might not lose a scholarship for drinking, but when teens drink, they do stupid things."

"Mom, you're being dramatic. One beer is nothing. Half my friends are—" He cut himself off short. No teenager was going to rat out his friends in front of the sheriff's department. Conner didn't need him to. He knew what went on at those parties. As an officer, he had broken up countless parties, including that one at Jason's house not long before he died.

"Were any of these kids at your house also at the party the night—" Grace lowered her voice, probably out of consideration for Conner, but it still stung "—Jason died?"

Charlie shrugged again and mumbled something that sounded a lot like, "I don't know."

"Give us a few names." Conner crossed his arms, trying to act casual, yet authoritative enough to demand some answers. What if one of these kids who had borrowed the Handlers' truck had tried to hurt Grace because she was getting too close to what really happened at the party the night Jason died? With the brand-new information from Levi that Jason wasn't drinking that night, it made it more imperative that Conner find out what really happened. *Had* someone drugged Jason's drink? If so, why? Had it been intentional, or had Jason picked up a drink intended for someone else?

A million questions swirled around his head, hurting his brain. He had to get to the bottom of it, for Jason. For Jason's mother. And for his own peace of mind.

"No one did anything. Come on," Charlie protested. Something akin to fear flashed in his eyes. What was he afraid of?

"How about I say a few names, and you tell me if they were drinking in your father's workshop?" Conner stuffed his hands into his jacket pockets, trying to act casual.

Charlie rolled his eyes in typical teenage fashion.

Conner made up a name and Charlie frowned. "No. I don't even know that kid. Does he live around here?" His tone suggested he thought Conner wasn't right in the head.

Conner didn't answer. "How about Bradley Poissant?"

"The mayor's son?" Jenny asked. She glared at her son. "Are you guys still friends?"

Charlie lifted one shoulder in a universal "whatever" gesture.

"Was Bradley there?" Levi had mentioned that Bradley and Jason were arguing the night Jason died. It didn't make sense. Bradley was a good kid. And the two teens were friends.

Charlie pushed off the arm of the couch and pleaded to his mom. "We weren't doing *anything*."

"Answer Captain Gates's question." Jenny planted her fists on her hips. "I'm not fooling around."

"Yeah, Bradley and a few other guys were here."

Conner stepped forward and clapped Charlie's shoulder. "Okay, thanks for being honest. I have no interest in getting you in trouble with your mom. If there's anything you need to tell me, tell me now."

"Charlie?" his mother silently urged her son to come clean with the officer. A genuine look of fear haunted her eyes.

"No, there's nothing else. Bradley was here with a few of his buddies. They're jerks, anyway. I haven't hung out with them since."

Jenny pulled her arms out of her winter coat and tossed it on the couch. She tugged at the collar of her sweater. "Charlie, I can't be at your side

24/7. You're going away to college. You have to be responsible. You've got to…" She fisted her hands and clenched her jaw. She turned to Conner. "What happens now?"

"Do you know who took the truck? Where did you keep the keys?"

"My dad always kept them in a key box in the workshop. And no, I don't know. If one of the guys took it, they did it without me knowing."

"Okay," Conner said, deciding to let that rest for now. "The sheriff's department will tow the truck off the Weavers' property as soon as they can get back there. See if the back-end damage matches the accident."

"That's fine. I don't care about the stupid truck. If Paul wants it, I'll tell him he can pick it up at the collision shop." Jenny scratched her head, as if trying to scrub the thought of her husband out of it. She took a step toward the door. "I have to get to work."

"I appreciate your time," Conner said, then turned to Charlie and handed him his business card. "If you think of anything else, call me."

Charlie took the card. A doubtful expression was plain on his face.

Once outside, Grace turned to Conner. "This Bradley Poissant's name has come up more than once. Maybe we should talk to him."

Unease sloshed in his gut. "I know Mayor Poissant and his family. They're good people. I can't believe he'd ram your car. It doesn't seem like him."

"People aren't always what they seem." She looked at him, and as much as he hated to acknowledge it, he agreed with her.

NINE

Later that afternoon, Grace watched Ruthie lumber down the stairs and lower herself into a rocking chair. "This baby can't come soon enough."

"How are you feeling?" Grace leaned forward on the matching rocker in the Hershbergers' sitting room. A cozy fire made her forget about the cold outside.

A hint of guilt reminded her that she hadn't been exactly honest with Conner. She had fully anticipated rereading all the articles surrounding her mother's murder in the *Quail Hollow Gazette* and spending the day at home. However, she'd stumbled upon the name Maryann Hershberger in one of the articles. Turned out Heather's right-hand employee at the bed & breakfast was none other than her daughter. Ruthie had stopped over to the bed & breakfast before Heather went on her honeymoon. Her sister had explained how Ruthie was the daughter of one of their mom's good friends from years ago. Once she had this piece of information, she had to take a drive to their home. Thankfully, her brother-in-law's truck made it out of the snowy yard.

"I'm doing fine. I'm curious how you're getting along at the bed & breakfast. It's a shame I couldn't fill in while your sister is away." She smiled. "This baby has other ideas." Ruthie had the glow of a woman excited about her first child.

"It's really no problem. It's given me a chance to get to know Quail Hollow a little bit better."

"You should stick around until spring. Then you'll really get a feel for the area. Everyone's cooped up inside now." Maryann, Ruthie's mother, didn't look up from her needlework, carefully drawing the needle and thread through the fabric.

Grace couldn't imagine herself in this small town much beyond her sister's return from her honeymoon. She couldn't even stay at the bed & breakfast for the afternoon without getting antsy.

"Ruthie's been spending more of her days here than at home," Maryann continued. "I think she's afraid of going into labor and not being able to track down her husband on one of his jobs."

"He's a handyman," Ruthie said proudly. "He did a lot of the work on the bed & breakfast."

"It's beautiful." Grace cleared her throat. "I hate to intrude on your peaceful afternoon," said Grace, finally deciding to broach the topic on her mind, "but I was looking into my mom's death."

Death sounded less bleak than *murder*. Everyone died. Only in truly awful cases did death come in the form of murder.

Maryann's head snapped up from her needlework. Then she immediately dipped it back down and seemed to struggle to get the needle through the fabric. Despite the older woman's obvious distress, Grace pressed on. "I read your name in one of the articles in the newspaper."

"I was a little girl then," Ruthie said, with an air of confusion. Then her eyes opened wide. "Oh, you mean *Mem. Mem* and Sarah were friends. Right?"

"Yah," Maryann said, a distant quality to her voice, perhaps lost in a pleasant memory. "We were." She smiled ruefully. "You and your sister resemble your *mem*."

"I regret that we never had any photos of her to remember her by," Grace said, wishing the room wasn't quite so warm.

"We don't believe in having photos. Yet the tourists don't seem to think anything of it nowadays. Always taking them." The older woman said *nowadays* with a longing for days gone by. The outside world was speeding up in a way Grace suspected Maryann could never imagine.

Grace blinked, thinking back to the photo someone had taken from a distance of her little family after their mother had been murdered. Even before the explosion of online news, local newspapers prided themselves on visual images. A photo like that would have sold a lot of papers.

The juxtaposition of the quiet Amish countryside with murder. The three grief-stricken girls left behind.

A familiar nagging worked at Grace, as if she were poking at a hornets' nest better left undisturbed. What did she hope to achieve, anyway?

"We were discouraged from talking to anyone back then," Maryann said. "The outsiders flooded Quail Hollow." She grew still. "What does the article say?"

"That you and my mom were friends. That you couldn't believe she was gone."

"Is that all?"

"Yes."

"True enough. I still can't believe she's gone, even after all these years." Maryann shook her bonneted head.

Grace opened her mouth to ask a question that had been on her mind, when Emma, Maryann's seventeen-year-old daughter, her youngest, came in through the kitchen and stomped her snowy boots on the floor mat.

"The greenhouse is okay." She smiled at her mom as she took off her coat. "We worried the heavy snow would crack the glass."

"Denki," Maryann said. "Now come in and get warm. This is Grace Miller, Heather's sister."

"Nice to meet you," Emma said shyly.

Ruthie groaned. "Emma, will you help me back upstairs? I need to lie down." She glanced at Grace. "Sorry, I'm not very good company."

"Oh, please, don't worry." Grace smiled, encouraged that maybe Maryann would be more receptive to talking about Sarah without her daughters around.

"Yah." Emma hung her coat on a hook near the fireplace to dry. "Want me to read to you some?"

Grace smiled, pondering a different life. Life with a *mem*, *dat* and two sisters in the quiet Amish community. A completely different upbringing from the one she'd had. Instead of reading books to each other, Heather, Grace and Rose tended to park themselves in front of the TV with frozen dinners while their dad picked up a second shift at the factory.

Emma held Ruthie's arm, helping her up the stairs. "Take care, Ruthie. I can't wait to meet that baby of yours."

Ruthie groaned and laughed. "Me, too. Me, too."

Grace rocked back and forth slowly, settling into the quietness of the place. For some reason, she felt content here with Maryann, whereas she was unsettled alone at the B&B. Perhaps she needed company.

"You're looking into Sarah's death?" Maryann asked, surprising Grace.

"I was looking into the underage drinking party. Then I got a little sidetracked when retired Sheriff Gates mentioned a relentless reporter who had covered my mom's death."

Maryann nodded. "I remember her. I shouldn't have spoken to her. She approached me in town. I was grief-stricken."

"You spoke from the heart. You and my mother were friends. And because of that long-ago conversation, I'm now talking to one of my mom's friends."

"True enough. Your *mem* and I *were* friends. *Gut* friends."

"Did my mom ever mention anything strange or unusual happening prior to her death? Something that had her worried?"

Sometimes people didn't realize they had valuable information. But Grace knew it was a long shot that Maryann would provide any new information after all these years.

"The sheriff asked me a lot of questions after Sarah's death." Maryann's eyes grew red-rimmed. "I was young. The loss was devastating."

"I'm sure you've thought a lot about my mom over the years. Did you ever remember something later that maybe was of significance?" Goosebumps blanketed Grace's skin, the same reaction she always got when she was about to get a huge lead in an investigation. It was nothing concrete. Just a feeling.

Maryann tilted her head, seemingly trying to discern if her daughters were within earshot.

Grace glanced up the stairs. She could hear the distant even cadence of a voice, someone reading. "Your daughters are close."

Maryann smiled sadly. "Your *mem* was like a sister to me. She was an only child, which is a rare thing among Amish families. We spent a lot of time together."

"What can you tell me about my mom? I hardly remember her."

Maryann gave Grace a sympathetic smile. "She was beautiful. Like you."

Grace leaned back in the rocking chair and let Maryann talk. The Amish woman touched the sides of her bonnet, a nervous gesture. "Before she married your *dat*, she had another suitor."

Grace smiled, having a hard time imagining her mom, younger than she was now, dating. "Do the Amish date a lot?" The longer Grace was in Quail Hollow, the more she realized how much she didn't know about her ancestry.

"He wasn't Amish." Maryann set aside her needlework and folded her hands in her lap.

Grace stifled a gasp. "Really?" What little fabric of her mother's life she thought she knew began to fray. A thread poked out at the edge. Did she dare pull it? "She dated an outsider?"

Maryann fidgeted with her hands, and pink splotches blossomed on her pale cheeks, suggesting she felt like she had betrayed her friend. "I'm not sure she was serious. I think a lot of Amish youth go through a rebellious phase. Some more than others." She angled her head when something sounded from the top of the stairs. She waited for a minute before continuing. "Your mother was happiest when she was corralling the three of you."

"Do you know who this man was?" Grace couldn't let Maryann gloss over this, even if it had nothing to do with her murder. "I mean, did my mom consider leaving the Amish?" Maybe Grace had painted a romantic notion of her father and mother that had never existed.

The conversation she'd had with the retired law enforcement officers came to mind. Her father had been a suspect. Had he been jealous? Heat pooled under her arms. Investigating her mother's death had been a mistake. Regardless of the outcome, she'd never be able to bottle up the questions that had escaped and now floated around her mind.

Maryann waved her hand, suggesting this new piece of information didn't matter. It was in the past, after all. "Oh, no. It was a harmless thing, I'm sure. Leaving the Amish would have devastated your *mammy*." Maryann tapped the pads of her fingers together. "Once your dad made his intentions known, she never talked of this *Englisch* boy again."

"She loved my father."

"Of course! Your father was a *gut* man."

Grace released a shaky breath she hadn't realized she'd been holding. By all accounts, her father had loved her mother dearly. After her father lost her mother, he had never recovered. He loved her. He had.

Relationships only lead to heartache.

The familiar refrain whispered across her brain.

Best to live her life on her own terms, traveling the world, giving a voice to the voiceless. Not getting attached.

Maryann stood and crossed over to where Grace sat in the rocker. The Amish woman's hand brushed across her shoulder. "Your mother was a dear friend. I'm here for her daughters."

"Thank you."

"Tell me, how is Rose? She was just a little thing when your mother died."

"She's doing well. She lives in Buffalo and has a great job as a midwife."

Maryann tilted her head to the side and smiled. "That's wonderful. I hope she is happy."

"She seems to be."

"Is she married? Kids?"

"Oh, no." It was Grace's turn to laugh. "Seems only Heather has taken that plunge."

Maryann's face grew somber. Grace sensed her mother's old friend wanted to ask her about her romantic relationships, so she spoke up first. "I suppose I should go."

"Wait, can I get you something?" Maryann asked.

"I'm fine. Thank you all the same." Grace drew in a deep breath. "Perhaps Emma would like to help out at the bed & breakfast for a bit now that Ruthie's going to have a family?" The idea had just come to Grace. The final decision would be up to Heather when she came back. But for now, Grace could use some temporary help. Dust didn't take a break during the off-season. Besides, the thought of company at the bed & breakfast cheered Grace. And maybe Emma knew some of the Amish teens who were at the party the night of Jason's death.

A concern wormed its way into Grace's subconscious. *Is everything about the story?*

Grace couldn't help herself. Stories were in her blood.

Just because the bishop ordered the youth to avoid the parties, didn't mean Emma would. Grace found that when something was forbidden, it became that much more desired. She hoped she could be a positive influence on the young woman. Tell her how to be smart and sidestep trouble if she found herself at parties.

"I'll go get her." Maryann stopped at the bottom of the stairs.

Grace got to her feet. "No, let me run up. If that's okay?"

"Yah." Maryann turned and continued into the kitchen.

Grace smiled and jogged up the stairs silently in her socks. Emma was still reading to her sister. Grace knocked quietly and then pushed open the door. Ruthie had drifted off to sleep while Emma seemed engrossed in the story.

"Hi," Grace whispered. Ruthie's breathing was even. "I don't want to wake your sister."

Understanding, Emma put a string in the book to mark her page and set it aside. They both stepped out into the hallway. "I wanted to know if you'd be interested in doing a little light cleaning at the bed & breakfast while I'm staying there?" Emma must wonder why a single woman couldn't clean up after herself.

"Yah. Yes," she corrected herself. "When?"

"Whenever works for you." She reached into her pocket and pulled out her business card, then realized how ridiculous that was. Her smile faded. "I was going to say you could call me."

Emma swiped the card from her hand. "We have a phone in the barn. We use it for business purposes. For the greenhouse. I'll come tomorrow."

"Sounds good." Grace glanced down the

stairs. Maryann didn't seem to be within earshot. "Can I ask you something?"

Emma twirled the strings of her bonnet, and her cheeks flared pink at the attention.

"Were you at the drinking party that made the news?"

Emma glanced around, appearing to be searching for an escape route. "You're the one writing a story."

"I am." She spoke encouragingly. "I promise not to get you into trouble."

Emma shook her head. "No, I wasn't at the party. I went right home after Sunday singing that night."

Grace decided not to press. She'd get to know the young woman soon enough when she came to work at the bed & breakfast.

"You have my card. See you tomorrow."

"Yah." Emma slipped back into Ruthie's room, and her steady voice picked up where she had left off in the story.

Grace had only been home long enough to formulate a blog post to keep her editor happy when she noticed a patrol car pulling up the driveway. Perhaps Conner had news about Bradley Poissant, the mayor's son.

She waited by the back door, hoping not to appear too eager. She counted to five after Conner's knock, and pulled the door open. Her greeting died on her lips. A female officer was standing next to Conner with a bag slung over her shoulder.

What's going on?

"Grace, this is Deputy Becky Spoth."

Grace backed up and hit her heel on the open door. "Hello, deputy."

"Mind if we come in?" Conner asked, amusement edging his tone. He must have noticed Grace's befuddlement.

"Um, sure. What's going on?" Grace stepped out of the way and the two officers came through the door, looking very official in their uniforms. "Does this mean you found the guy who rammed me at the gas station?" What other reason would Conner have for bringing Deputy Spoth with him? What was with the bag?

Conner hooked his thumbs in his belt. "Sorry to say we couldn't locate Bradley. The mayor said he was away on a college visit with his mom. Just for today. We don't even know he was involved, but until we arrest who was, I'd prefer if you weren't alone out here."

"Do you think it was Bradley?" Grace's gaze drifted to Conner then the deputy and back. She was sensing he was having doubts.

Conner took off his hat and scratched his head. "It's a stretch. I've known the mayor a long time. I've known Bradley his entire life. He's a good kid. Made a mistake drinking out back behind

Jason's house. His parents were grateful to know what their son was up to. He's on the straight and narrow now."

"You trust him that much?" Grace leaned back and gripped the counter behind her. "But that's not the end of it, right? Did you find out why he was arguing with Jason? Does the mayor know why you're looking for him?"

"We had to tell him something. I told him I had questions regarding the party. That I heard he was there with Jason," Conner said. "For all he knows, he thinks I want to know more about Jason's last hours, being family and all. And as far as the fighting, kids argue, right?"

"Sounds like you've talked yourself into this theory." Grace watched him closely. A shadow crossed his face, suggesting perhaps she was right.

"The mayor seemed pretty wrecked about Jason's death," Deputy Spoth added, looking toward Conner for confirmation. "It's a sad situation. After the boys were caught drinking at Jason's, Bradley lost his starting position as quarterback—part of school district policy if caught with drugs or alcohol. He said his son realized it was a wake-up call."

"To a teenage kid, missing out on a big game is a big deal. It was perhaps the end of his football career." Although Grace didn't have kids, she had heard more times than she could count that teenage brains weren't fully developed. That they did stupid things for stupid reasons. Acted irrationally. The officers had to know that better than anyone.

"I'd hardly call it a career," Conner scoffed. "His parents said he had no plans to play past high school. They looked forward to the day he hung up his cleats. The game's tough. Don't go grasping for reasons for him to get revenge on Jason that don't exist."

"Why are you shutting me down?"

"I know these people." Conner leveled an even gaze at her. "They've known Jason a long time. They want to know the truth, too."

"Not if it means taking their son down."

Conner pressed his hands together and touched the tips of his fingers to his lips. "Okay, I'll do a little more digging."

"Thank you," Grace said, and pushed off the counter. "Now, about Deputy Spoth staying with me?" She pointed at Deputy Spoth's bag.

"You didn't run this by her ahead of time?" The deputy shook her head, giving Conner a skeptical look. Already Grace liked this woman.

"You need protection out here," Conner said as if that trumped everything.

Grace was beginning to miss her quiet hotel rooms in various cities where she could come and go without everyone worrying about her. "I thought we've been over this. I have the alarm."

She sighed. "I won't forget to turn it on if Boots comes knocking." If only she hadn't forgotten that one step, she wouldn't be stuck entertaining this sheriff's deputy.

"I'd feel better if you had more than an alarm. I got authorization to have Deputy Becky Spoth stay with you."

Grace squared her shoulders. "No offense, deputy, but I don't need a babysitter."

"Please, call me Becky." Self-consciously, she touched one of the long braids pinned on top of her head.

Grace was beginning to feel a bit like a heel, but Conner had given her no choice.

"Humor me." A slow smile crept up Conner's face, and Grace's heart melted. *Traitorous heart!* If she stayed in Quail Hollow much longer, she'd be in jeopardy, and not only from some testosterone-fueled punk in a big truck.

Grace held up her hands, too tired to argue.

Conner took a step, retreating toward the door. "I have to follow up on a few things. You going to be okay?"

"Sure," the two women said in unison, then looked at each other. Grace smiled, figuring the young deputy probably didn't want to be here any more than she wanted a babysitter.

Once Conner stepped outside, the deputy moved to the door and locked it. "What's the code for the alarm?"

Grace told her, and the deputy set it. "I'm sure they'll track down whoever is harassing you, and then your life will go back to normal."

Grace was beginning to wonder what normal looked like. She had never had a normal life.

Grace opened the fridge and stared inside at the expired quart of half-and-half as well as a bruised apple and a withered pear left over from the fruit basket Rose had sent. She had hoped something good to eat would spontaneously appear. If she were here alone, she'd probably eat a granola bar or a bowl of cereal. *I wonder if my guest would enjoy that?*

Grace turned around and planted her fists on her hips. "You hungry? We could order takeout."

"No one will deliver out here." Becky strolled over and pointed at a door off the kitchen. "Pantry?"

Grace nodded. Her sister had mentioned the pantry, but Grace hadn't even opened it. She wasn't much of a cook.

Becky opened the door of the well-stocked pantry and studied its contents. "I can whip something up."

"Really?" Grace glanced over the deputy's shoulder at the cans, jars and containers that struck her more like a last resort during a snowstorm, when you were willing to risk botulism versus starving to death. "My sister had an Amish woman run her kitchen."

Earlier today she had watched Emma helping a very pregnant Ruthie up the stairs. Grace reached in and read a date on the can, but they hadn't come from any manufacturer. The Amish must have canned the food. "Hmm…she must have stocked up before she went on maternity leave. I never thought to look in there for something to eat." Living on the road always meant eating out. Since her sister left, she had been living on a few fresh foods stored in the fridge, cold cereal, granola bars and prepared food she had picked up in town. She wasn't fussy.

The deputy gave her a strange look and laughed quietly to herself. She undid the buttons on her cuffs and rolled back her sleeves. "If it's okay with you, I'll make us something for dinner. I promise you it'll be good."

"Sure." Grace hoped the single word of agreement didn't show her doubt. "What can I do?"

The deputy handed her a basket of potatoes. "You can peel these while I see what vegetables you have."

The two women worked in companionable silence. Grace never realized that peeling potatoes could be a nice distraction. Becky, as the deputy insisted on being called, finished preparing the meal, and the two of them sat down at the table to eat something that resembled Shepherd's Pie. Grace had to clear the paperwork and her computer from the table.

Grace took a bite, and the flavor exploded in her mouth. It took her back. Made her think of home.

A home she had lost the day her mother was murdered.

"Where did you learn to cook like this? It reminds me of my childhood." Grace wasn't even sure that was possible. Her mom had died when she was three, and her dad had moved his young family away shortly after.

A small smile hooked the corner of the deputy's mouth. The young woman had a flawless beauty, and Grace suspected she wasn't wearing any makeup. "I grew up Amish."

Grace laughed. "Really? I did, too. Well, not really. I left a long time ago."

"I know," Becky said. Of course she knew. "I'm sorry. I didn't mean to offend you. Everyone who grew up around here knows about your *mem*." It was strange to hear Pennsylvania Dutch coming from the deputy's mouth.

"How old were you when you left?" Grace took another bite. "This is really good," she added quickly, pointing at the food with her fork.

"Thanks." Becky seemed pleased, as if she hadn't cooked for anyone in a long time. "I left when I was seventeen."

"Did you leave all by yourself?"

Becky swallowed and smiled ruefully. "Yes."

"Yet you stayed in Quail Hollow?"

"Call me a glutton for punishment." Becky dragged a fork through her mashed potatoes, making Grace think about how she had done the same when she was a child. She liked to pretend she was paving roads through the mountainside in her mashed potatoes. "It's not too bad. I still have family here."

Grace suspected this was the true reason the young woman had stayed in town despite leaving the Amish faith.

"They're okay with…" Grace held out her hand to the uniform, indicating the life of an *Englischer*.

"No, my parents are disappointed. They didn't have to shun me because I left before I was baptized, but I'm certainly not welcome at home." Her voice grew soft. "They consider me a bad influence on my sister."

"Please forgive me if I'm overstepping for asking this question. Wouldn't it be easier to move away?" Grace folded a corner of the napkin and ran her finger over the fold. "Make a clean break?" That's why Grace suspected her father had left. Easier to move on from the past if it wasn't always poking you smack between the eyes. If truth be told, her father had never moved on. He'd gone through the motions, providing for his family, until he suffered an early death.

Becky dipped her head, and her cheeks grew feverish. "I don't know much beyond Quail Hollow. When I decided to leave the Amish, a woman who lives about thirty minutes away took me in. She helps other youth who decide to leave. I caught up with my education and took classes at the community college."

Grace took another bite of her potatoes, allowing Becky to talk. Grace had never considered that there would be people who helped in the transition of runaway Amish. "How did you end up back here?"

"After community college, I looked for a job. Admittedly, I didn't look far. The first job I was offered was in the sheriff's department. One thing led to another, and I eventually became a deputy."

"Interesting."

"The sheriff thought perhaps I'd be able to form a bridge between law enforcement and the Amish. However, the Amish are as skeptical of law enforcement today as they ever were. Maybe more so."

"That's got to be tough."

"Many people lead tough lives." Becky covered Grace's hand, her gaze reaching inside her soul. "There are far worse things than living in a town where the majority of the residents think calling you a fence jumper is going to hurt your feelings."

"Fence jumper?" Grace asked, curious.

"Yes, someone who left the Amish." Her eyes twinkled in amusement.

Grace scooped up more mashed potatoes. "From one fence jumper to another, this is awesome." Maybe having a bodyguard wouldn't be so bad.

If only Grace and Conner could figure out who wanted her to leave the Amish community again, once and for all.

TEN

After finishing his shift, Conner changed into shorts and a T-shirt and made his way to the small room in the sheriff's department designated for physical fitness. He started running, hoping hard footfalls on the relentless conveyor could beat the frustration out of him. He couldn't wait for the snow to melt. Then he could run his usual three-mile course along the country roads, up hills, alongside fields and barns and past buggies and wagons. There was something therapeutic about it. However, until the snow melted, he'd have to settle for the treadmill and the local news coming out of Buffalo on the small screen in front of him.

Thankfully, the wild-party clips from the news stations had died down, even though Conner was generating more questions in his own investigation on that exact same story. He hoped the answers he uncovered didn't generate another cycle of news stories. This evening, the news anchors were spending an inordinate amount of time discussing the weather. Nothing novel about that. A snowstorm warning was in effect for tomorrow, bringing a potential nine inches of the white fluffy stuff.

That meant more time on the treadmill.

Just great.

Annoyed, Conner snapped off the TV and jammed his earbuds, connected to his phone balanced precariously on the tray in front of him, into his ears. Arms pumping, he got into a rhythm. All the conversations he had had over the course of the past few days bounced around his head. Despite all his protests to the contrary, he couldn't shake Grace's concerns. *Was* he overlooking Bradley because the case was too personal?

He wiped sweat off his brow and allowed his mind to drift back to the night he had received a call from Anna, Jason's mother. She thought Jason and his friends were out back drinking. A visit from the sheriff's department would set them straight.

Sure enough, when Conner arrived, a few guys were pounding back beers. After seeing that each of the young men made it safely home, Conner took it upon himself to follow up with their parents. Perhaps his first mistake was not following through more with Jason. Conner had no idea that his actions would have a domino effect, getting the mayor's son suspended from the football team and effectively ending the small town's run in the playoffs.

Was the mayor dismissing how big of a deal that missed opportunity really was? Again, had Conner allowed his friendship with the mayor to cloud his judgment regarding his son?

Bam-bam-bam.

The soles of his shoes slapped the conveyor belt, sending a jolt through his entire body.

Could Jason's best friend really have lashed out at him? Drugged his drink to mess with him, not grasping the true danger? Not realizing that Jason would get behind the wheel of a truck and kill himself and seriously injure a young Amish woman?

Bam-bam-bam.

His footsteps landed heavily on the treadmill belt. He turned the music up in his ears, trying to drown out his thoughts. Could Conner have been that blind?

If this kid was desperate enough to drug someone for payback, what would he do to a reporter trying to uncover the truth?

Despite cranking his music up mind-numbingly loud, Conner still couldn't turn off his thoughts.

Bam-bam-bam.

Exertion usually helped Conner calm down.

Not tonight. His frustration was ramping up with his heartbeat.

He hated punks. He hated being duped.

Conner swiped the back of his hand across his sweaty forehead. He'd have to come up with a plan. He knew he couldn't keep Grace under his watch—or the watch of a fellow officer— forever. Grace was much too independent. First chance she got, she'd be back out there, asking more questions.

Questions that someone obviously didn't want her to find answers to.

Arms and legs pumping, music cranking, thoughts swirling, Conner pretended he was outside, climbing the crest of the road winding through the cornfields. If only he was smelling the country air and not whatever greasy mess one of his coworkers had warmed up in the microwave in the nearby break room.

A shadow crossed his line of vision, and Conner pulled out an earbud, then the other. Heavy breaths from his exertion sounded loud in his ears. He didn't try to pivot to see who was there because then he'd have to break his stride or risk flying off the treadmill. There were too many cameras situated around this place to risk that. He was not about to become a viral video.

"Captain Gates." The sheriff's commanding tone was unmistakable.

Conner hit the stop button and grabbed the

handlebars as the treadmill came to an abrupt stop. Forget the usual cooldown. He grabbed the edge of his T-shirt and wiped his forehead, a preemptive effort to prevent the sweat from stinging his eyes.

Conner gave his boss, dressed in a crisp uniform, a sly smile. "I find I get a better workout if I change out of uniform."

The sheriff stared back at him, clearly not amused. "We need to talk."

Conner stepped down from the platform. His legs vibrated from the sudden ceasing of motion. He wiped his forehead again. "How can I help you?"

"The mayor called."

Conner got a sinking feeling and waited for the sheriff to continue.

"What's your endgame?"

Conner leaned forward and planted his hands on his thighs, trying to catch his breath. He angled his head to look up at the sheriff. "I'm trying to understand what happened the night Jason died. I have new information that suggests he wasn't drinking or doing drugs. That maybe he was drugged."

The sheriff faltered for a moment before continuing. "You have to let it go. Jason's death was a tragic accident." The sheriff shook his head. "These other kids feel awful that they didn't stop him from drinking, doing drugs, and driving."

Conner could feel a muscle working in his jaw. Something didn't make sense.

The sheriff pinned him with his gaze. "Maybe you need to take some time off."

Conner froze and straightened. He plucked his damp T-shirt away from his chest. "What?"

"You've been working long hours. You lost your cousin, then his son in a short period of time. Take a week off. Pull yourself together."

"What am I supposed to do with a week off in the middle of winter?"

The sheriff curled his hand and tapped his fist on one of the treadmill's rails. "I've made my decision. I don't want to see you back here until next week."

Conner swiped his towel from where he had draped it over an unused piece of equipment. The first twinges of a headache hammered behind his eyes. "See you next week," Conner gritted out as he stormed from the workout area, afraid if he said anything more he'd be out of a job for far longer than a week.

Conner showered at the sheriff's department, changed into street clothes and drove over to see Anna Klein. This unexpected week off might give him the time he needed to finally get some answers. He doubted that was the sheriff's intent, but that was Conner's plan.

When he reached his cousin's wife's house, it

was dark. It was too early for someone to be in bed but not too early for someone who had lost everything to be taking a nap or doing something to otherwise make herself forget.

But Anna had never been much of a drinker and certainly not a drug user. Neither had his cousin Ben; that's why it had come as such a blow that their son had driven under the influence.

From the front stoop, he could hear music. It only took him a couple notes to recognize the Buffalo band that had made it big. A band he and his cousin had taken more than one road trip to see.

Sorry I let you down, buddy. I didn't do right by your son.

If for no other reason, Conner owed his deceased cousin answers about his dead son, and Conner wouldn't stop until he had them.

What a nightmare.

Conner drew in a deep breath and knocked. After a few seconds, the music cut off and then the curtain on the door pulled back. Anna gave him a lopsided smile and dropped the curtain. She released the dead bolt and opened the door.

Anna ran a hand over her mussed hair. "I wasn't expecting anyone."

"Sorry." He hadn't given her a call in advance because he feared she'd beg off from a visit, and he needed to ask her some questions about Jason's relationship with Bradley.

Anna led the way to the family room. She turned on a light as she passed and lifted up the remote from the couch cushion to place it on the coffee table. The image of her lying in the dark listening to music was more than he could bear. What would his cousin think about his heartbroken bride?

"How are you doing?"

"How do you think I'm doing?" He could see it all in her haunted expression.

"I need to ask you a few questions." Conner got right to it. "Did Jason suffer any backlash after the party I broke up here?"

Anna sat down on the edge of the couch, sinking into the soft cushions. She held up the palms of her hands. "How would I know? I'm his mom… The mom is the last to know." Her words had a sad resignation to them.

"How did he seem after the bonfire here?"

"Moody. That's to be expected, right? His mom called the sheriff's department on his party."

Conner sat down on the coffee table near her and touched her hand. "It's not like you called 9-1-1. You called me. I'm family."

"Family in the sheriff's department." Anna sighed heavily. "I'm not sorry I called you." She frowned, and a silent tear trailed down her cheek.

"I'm thinking I didn't call you enough. My kid was out of control and I couldn't stop him."

"You can't beat yourself up over this." If only Conner could take his own advice.

She picked up a decorative pillow and held it to her midsection. "I've got nothing else to do but think and analyze and wonder what else I could have done." She started to push to her feet, offering him something to eat or drink.

"No, no. Sit…"

She plopped back down and met his gaze. He had been a bit envious of his cousin Ben, who was ten years older, when he met Anna and had a son. They seemed to have the perfect family, unlike the broken home he had come from.

Now look at what remained of that perfect family.

Conner was cynical about relationships. Too much potential heartache.

"What is it?" The look in Anna's eyes suggested there wasn't much more she could hear that would faze her. She had already lost everything that was important to her.

"I heard some rumblings that Jason and Bradley had a run-in the night Jason died," Conner confided in her. "Had they been on the outs?"

"I don't know. I mean…" Her eyes moved quickly back and forth, searching her memory. "Kids go through phases. Bradley and Jason were joined at the hip growing up. They had other friends, too. I never thought much of it. Boys don't have the drama that girls usually do, or so I've heard." Anna dragged a hand across her tired face. Grief had aged her in the past year.

"I guess not." Conner glanced around at the small space. In the corner near the back sliding door to the deck, he noticed a pair of sneakers. Based on the size and style, they had to belong to her deceased son. One shoe was tipped on its side.

He turned back to Anna, realizing she wasn't going to provide him with any new information on her son's relationship with Bradley. "Is there anything I can do for you?"

She sat upright and stretched to drag the laptop that was sitting on the far end of the coffee table closer to her. "Maybe there is." She flipped open the laptop, and a professional photo of Grace smiled back at him. "Maybe you can get this lady to stop writing about Jason."

Conner spun the computer around to face him. He skimmed the blog entry dated today.

I never intended to be in Quail Hollow for this long. Maybe it's part of God's plan. My life started in Quail Hollow, then tragedy pulled me away. I've often fantasized about what my life might have been if I'd grown up Amish, yet I resisted coming back to face my past. To see what I had lost.

Now that I'm here, I've been blessed to meet people who knew my mother when she was younger than I am now. That's hard to believe. And I've learned that the Amish can have complicated lives, despite trying to live simply.

And, tragically, I've learned that despite their attempted isolation, drugs and alcohol can play a deadly role in their lives. You can't share the same stores, restaurants and roads without crossing paths with exactly what you're trying to avoid.

That was never more apparent than a fateful autumn night when a young man named Jason Klein, an *Englischer* as the Amish call them, clipped his truck on the wagon of Katy Weaver, a young Amish woman.

But the longer I'm here, the more I'm discovering answers aren't always black-and-white. Sometimes there are shades of gray. I'm determined to find those answers before life calls me to my next location.

Hopefully someplace without snow.

Conner snapped the lid of the computer closed, a failed attempt to keep his anger in check. How could Grace still be writing about Jason after everything they'd learned? After he warned her that she was putting herself in jeopardy?

"I'll talk to Grace."

Anna nodded. "I thought you might know her. People in town said you were hanging around with a reporter." Conner detected a hint of disappointment in her tone.

"It's not exactly what you think." He had a job to do. He had to protect Grace.

The smile on Anna's lips didn't reach her eyes. "I'm hoping I can find peace if people stop hounding me." She placed her hand on top of the laptop. "Someone from a Buffalo news station called, asking me to comment on those posts." She pulled her shoulders forward in a shrug. "I can't stop reading her posts. Punishing myself." She dragged a hand through her hair. "I need her to stop posting things about the accident."

Conner placed a hand on Anna's shoulder. "I'll take care of it." He had made a promise to Ben and failed him. Now, protecting Ben's wife from further pain was a promise Conner was determined to keep.

Early the next morning, a loud knock on the back door made Grace jump. The sight of Conner's personal truck calmed her nerves.

"That man has got to learn to call," she muttered as she placed a hand over her thundering chest.

She glanced up at the clock.

Why isn't he at work?

Becky had left a full hour ago for the start of

her shift. She wanted to make it into work before the forecasted snowstorm hit. It made Grace wonder who was paying her for her overnight shift. It didn't seem likely the sheriff's department would put Grace's safety ahead of keeping their overtime budget in check.

Not her problem, she supposed.

She lowered the lid to her laptop, slid off the bench and stretched her back. The smile slid from her face when she opened the door and saw Conner's stern expression. He seemed strung tight, and his muscles twitched in his jaw.

"What's wrong?"

He hesitated a fraction of a second, as if waiting for an invitation, then when he didn't get it, he pushed past her. "I thought we had an agreement."

She held up her palms in confusion. "What are you talking about?"

He strode over to her laptop and jabbed his finger at it. "What were you doing just now?"

Conner had shown himself to always be a gentleman, but she had never seen this side of him. In the blink of an eye, she was a teenager hiding in the closet while her brother-in-law screamed at her sister.

An icy pool of dread settled in her stomach, and she took a step back and squared her shoulders. Conner must have seen her reaction, and he relaxed his posture and lowered his voice.

"Listen, you have the right to do whatever you please. However…" He pointed at her laptop again. "This is not helping."

"*This* is my job." She reached around him and tapped the lid of her laptop for emphasis.

Conner sat down slowly on the bench. "I saw Jason's mom last night."

Grace crossed her arms and leaned against the wall. "Oh?"

"She's been following your blog." He lifted his eyes to hers. "It's causing her more pain."

"My editor is pressuring me to push forward with the story. Did you read my recent post?"

"Yeah."

"I didn't say anything that would jeopardize the investigation. I thought it was rather masterful how I touched on current events without giving anything away." She tipped her head and lifted her eyes, seeking his approval.

"People are finding your posts and then calling Anna for comment."

"I'm sorry." She really was, but she wanted to keep her job. "Maybe Anna could get an unlisted number." She ran a hand across her eyes, which were gritty from staying up late last night, rereading all the articles that had been written about her mother's murder. No matter how many times she read them, nothing struck her as new.

Because there *was* nothing new.

Except for the information that Mrs. Hershberger had shared. An outsider had been courting her mother before she married her father.

She sat down on the kitchen bench and glanced at Conner. She should probably be focusing on one story or the other, but her head told her this could be something bigger, the combination of an accident on a lonely road between a wagon and a truck and the murder of an Amish woman almost three decades ago. There were probably countless incidences—many far less newsworthy—that would make a fascinating read of the true-life stories of the Amish.

Yet her compassionate side told her it might be too revealing. What would her parents think? Even though they had both been dead for a long time now, she often guided her life by imagining what they would do. It kept her honest.

Most of the time.

"I'll be more thoughtful in the future," she finally said.

Conner nodded and unzipped his jacket, but didn't press her for more concrete promises. He probably knew her too well.

"Why aren't you at work?"

"Funny story."

"What?"

He shifted, his thigh accidentally brushing against hers. "I'm on forced vacation."

Grace's hand flew to her mouth. "On account of me? Oh, I hope not."

He ran his hands up and down his thighs. "The mayor called the sheriff. Suggested I was too close to the case."

"I thought everything was okay when you talked to the mayor?" Her pulse whooshed louder in her ears. "Maybe their son isn't innocent." Excitement edged her tone. She couldn't help herself.

Conner cut her a sideways glance. "Can we let it rest? For five seconds, maybe?"

"Okay. Can I ask you something about my mother's murder investigation, then?"

"Sure."

Grace's cell phone rang at that exact moment. Before completely ignoring the call, she checked caller ID. It was a local area code. Curious, she held up her finger. "Excuse me a second."

Emma Hershberger was on the other end of the line, asking if it was okay if she came over another day to help out because of the snow.

"Of course," Grace said into the phone. "Call me the next time you have a free day and it's not snowing."

She ended the call and turned back to Conner. "Sorry about that. I wanted to ask you if Harry ever mentioned investigating any old boyfriends of my mother's?"

"I was a kid. I heard bits and pieces. My dad didn't discuss the details of the case with me.

I'm sure he'd be willing to discuss it with you again, if you'd like."

"It's such a random angle. Something that Emma's mom said got me thinking. Mrs. Hershberger and my mom were good friends." She ran a hand over her mouth. "It's probably a dead end, but one I'd like to ask the retired sheriff about."

"Okay…" He planted his hands on his thighs and stood. "And you'll hold off on the blog. Until—"

"Until? There will never be a time that this tragedy won't hurt Jason's mom. It doesn't matter if I write about it or not, she'll still be hurting. Except maybe if I—if *we*—ask enough questions, she'll have answers to what really happened. Answers I never had regarding my mother's death."

"You can justify this any way you want. Anna is hurting now. I need to help her."

"I feel bad for Anna. I've kept her in my prayers," Grace said softly.

"How can you have faith after everything you've been through?"

"How can I not?"

Conner seemed to study her for a long minute before taking her hand and threading his fingers through hers. Warmth raced up her arm. Staring at their entwined fingers, her chest grew tight. "I'm on your side. Really, I am." He kissed the back of her hand. "I'm worried about your safety."

Grace pulled her hand away from his lips, but not out of his clasp. "Why are you so worried?"

A deep line creased his forehead. "What do you mean? Someone's harassing you."

She slid her hand out of his and stood. "You've gone above and beyond for me. You've put your job on the line." She lowered her head. "Why? You can't possibly do this for everybody." Her heart raced in her ears as she held her breath, waiting for his answer.

Conner searched her face in a way that made Grace very self-aware. Too self-aware. She shook her head and added, "Never mind, I shouldn't have asked."

He reached out and touched her elbow, the whisper of a touch that sent waves of awareness coursing through her. "No, you have every right to ask. It's something I've had to ask myself." A hint of a smile touched his eyes. "You've gotten under my skin."

She raised her eyebrows and her face grew warm. She didn't know how to respond to that.

Conner rubbed his forehead, obviously second guessing his confession. "I shouldn't have crossed the line. My job is to protect you."

"You didn't cross the line." She finally found her voice. "I'm only in Quail Hollow temporarily. My job has me traveling the world." The words felt like an excuse. For the first time in her adult life, the thought of planting roots didn't seem like such a crazy idea.

But what about Dad's heartbreak when Mom died? Heather's pain when her husband turned abusive?

Grace sat back down slowly. "I'm not in a position to date anyone." She looked up to meet his gaze. "Don't take it personally."

A light came into his eyes and he laughed. "Hard not to take it personally. But I do understand." He took a step backward toward the door, as if to make a hasty retreat. "I'm pretty much a confirmed bachelor." He shrugged. "I didn't exactly have the best role models while growing up. My dad was a workaholic and my mother bailed when I was just a kid."

Grace caught a glimpse of the hurt little boy in his wry expression. "I'm sorry. I didn't know that." A part of her felt guilty. Everything about their relationship had been about her. Grace knew far less about him. "Do you stay in touch with your mother?"

He shook his head. "She moved on. New husband. New kids."

She pushed to her feet and approached him. She looked in one eye then the other. Mustering courage she didn't realize she had, she reached out and cupped his smooth cheek. "I'm sorry."

"It was a lifetime ago."

"We both know that time doesn't heal all

wounds." She leaned in and brushed a kiss across his warm lips. Fearing she'd never be this brave again, she tried to memorize the moment.

ELEVEN

Conner ran his hand down Grace's long silky hair and she blinked slowly. Time didn't heal all wounds, but this woman just might. The realization surprised him. He cleared his throat. "Despite our determination to both stay single, I'm curious, have you ever thought you could be happy in Quail Hollow?"

"I'm happy now." A light shone in her eyes, then she suddenly looked down, but didn't step away from him. "My mother's death broke my father." She shook her head, as if trying to dismiss some horrible memory. "And I saw first-hand how wrong relationships can go with my sister and her first husband. I just…" She looked up and met his gaze. "I'm not cut out for this. I'm content traveling and writing. That's all I need."

He wondered if she were trying to convince herself.

"But if I was looking to stay in some really cold, snowy place, Quail Hollow would be the top of my list." She laughed, obviously trying to lighten the mood.

Conner tucked a strand of her hair behind her ear, deciding not to push the topic. He didn't want to scare her away. "Perhaps if we were two different people with very different pasts."

"Perhaps…" They stared into one another's eyes for a long moment, then she said, "We should probably focus on the task at hand."

"I suppose you're right." Maybe at another point in time they'd be willing to explore whatever was going on between them.

She shifted away from him. Immediately, he missed the fragrance of her hair. The warmth of her proximity.

But she was right. They had work to do.

Grace filled the teakettle at the sink. "You mentioned you talked to Anna last night," she said, getting right down to business, and the warm and cozy mood that had surrounded them dissipated.

"Did Anna indicate if Jason and Bradley had been in a fight the night of the party?" Grace continued.

"She didn't know."

Grace reached for two mugs and set them on the counter with a clank. "Pretend you don't have a personal relationship with Bradley. Do you think he is in any way capable of ramming a truck into my car? That's pretty violent behavior."

His stomach sunk and he shook his head. "I don't."

"What about breaking into the bed & breakfast to scare me?"

"I can't imagine any of it. And, most of all, I can't imagine Bradley drugging Jason. They grew up together."

Grace turned around and grabbed two tea bags from the cupboard, tore them open, then placed one in each mug. She leaned back against the counter, apparently to wait for the water to boil.

"Keeping emotions out of it, let's think logically," she said. Conner had been down the logical road and hadn't liked what he'd seen. "Bradley gets in trouble for drinking at Jason's house, ruins his dreams of winning a state title in football and, despite what his parents claim, he *is* mad. Really mad. This was supposed to be his moment of glory. Star quarterback. Big game." She screwed up her face, thinking. "A lot of people peak in high school. That game could have been a story Bradley told for the rest of his life. Instead, he gets in trouble for drinking and he's done. School policy. So—" her eyes grew bright "—he decides to have a little payback. He spikes the drink of the kid who got him in trouble. Show that Jason, cousin of Captain Gates of the sheriff's department, is not a Goody Two-shoes like he claims to be."

"Jason didn't call the sheriff's department. His mother did."

"Doesn't matter. In the eyes of a teenager, Jason's at fault. And what better way to show his mother that Jason's not such a good kid than by sending him home drugged up? A nice reminder to his mother to keep her nose out of their business."

"Isn't that a huge risk to take? Look what happened."

"Bradley didn't think through all the ramifications."

"If he drugged Jason, why not stop there, especially after the horrific consequences? Pray to God for forgiveness and that no one ever finds out and then move on with your life."

Grace's eyes widened. "That's exactly it." And Conner knew it, too. "He can't stop. Not now. He has to make sure no one ever finds out he's responsible for the accident. Whatever hopes he had for his future—football or not—would be destroyed."

"Maybe…" Conner still wasn't ready to believe Bradley Poissant was guilty of all that. "But why come after you? I've been investigating, too."

"Don't you see? He knows you'd never suspect him. You said it yourself. You've known him since he was a boy. He was Jason's friend. His best friend. Even now, you're doubting it's possible."

"We work on more than theories. We need proof."

"Yes, and I'm the writer in town, investigating the night of the accident. I'm the one he needs to stop."

"Now I can tell why you're a writer."

The kettle whistled and Grace spun around to fill the two mugs. She carried them over and sat down next to Conner. "Too out there?"

He pulled his tea bag out of the mug and set it on the napkin. "I wish it was. In this line of work, I've seen how dark people's hearts can be. I never imagined Bradley had it in him." He took a long sip of the piping-hot tea. "But even at that, we need proof. If he is involved, he's only digging himself in deeper."

Grace tapped her fingers on the table. "You're officially off duty because you're too close to Jason's case." Staring off in the yard, her eyes tracked something only she could see. She seemed to be plotting something.

"Yeah, and probably because I'm too close to you." He lowered his gaze to her mouth, and her breath hitched. He shifted in his seat and took a long sip of the tea. If he wanted to solve this case and respect her wishes, he'd have to check his emotions. She had made it clear she wasn't going to stay in Quail Hollow long term. And, quite frankly, why did he think their relationship wouldn't eventually implode? All his previous relationships had.

The corner of her pink mouth quirked into a grin. "Vacation, huh? What are you going to do with all your free time?"

"Make sure you don't get in trouble." He glanced around. "Where's Becky?"

"She left for work. My understanding is that she only had to guard me overnight. Make sure someone didn't murder me in my sleep." Grace laughed nervously.

"Nothing's going to happen to you. Not while I'm around." He still didn't like Grace out here all alone, day or night. This forced vacation meant he could protect her during the day.

She jerked her head back, and a strand of hair fell over her forehead. He resisted the urge to push it off her face. Her expression grew serious. "I appreciate your being here for me. I'm used to going it alone."

"You don't have to anymore." He wrapped the napkin around the teabag and stood. He tossed it into the garbage can. "Why don't we track Bradley down? See what he has to say?"

"Now?"

"Sure, the schools are closed because of the snow. We might get lucky and catch him at home."

Grace ran upstairs to grab a sweater out of her dresser, stuffing her arms into the sleeves as she walked briskly toward the bathroom. She snatched her lip gloss off the glass shelf and caught her reflection in the mirror.

She stopped and stared. A hint of a shadow lingered under her eyes. She had lost a lot of sleep lately between her illness and the two cases she had been investigating.

"Make sure you dress warmly," Conner hollered from the bottom of the stairs.

"Okay." She peered out the window. The falling snow was blanketing all the out buildings. The new red-stained barn with accents of snow could have been a postcard photo.

Mem's body was found in the old barn.

For a woman who left Quail Hollow at age three, there were far too many haunting memories. She couldn't stay here despite her growing feelings for Conner. And a short-term romance wouldn't be fair to either of them. When Grace made all her life plans—writing and traveling the world—she had never imagined meeting a man as kind as Conner.

Hadn't Heather once thought Brian was nice?

Grace grabbed a fastener off her dresser and twirled her hair into a messy bun. She grabbed a hat and gloves out of the closet, then turned to run back downstairs.

Focus on the investigation.

That was the safest thing to do for everyone.

"The house is up here on the right," Conner said distractedly while adjusting the windshield wipers in a futile attempt to keep up with the driving snow.

"Are you sure this is a good idea?" Grace's sudden apprehension did nothing to squash the little critter of doubt scurrying around Conner's brain, making him wonder if it was a good idea to pay Bradley Poissant a little visit. "Are you sure neither of his parents are home?" She leaned forward against the seat belt and squinted out the windshield.

"I called the mayor's office. The mayor is there, making sure all services are being provided during the storm. And since schools have been cancelled for the day, there's a good chance we can catch Bradley at home."

"What about his mom?"

"Also at work. I checked," Conner said. Mrs. Poissant was an insurance agent at some office just outside of Quail Hollow. Probably not very busy on a day like today. "If we catch Bradley at home, we'll chat unofficially, since I'm technically on vacation. And Bradley's eighteen." Conner wasn't sure who he was trying to convince.

A cautionary voice grew louder, warning him that what he was doing could blow up in his face.

Would *surely* blow up in his face.

His father, the retired sheriff, certainly wouldn't approve. He dismissed the thought. Conner was his own man. He'd deal with whatever fallout came his way. He had to follow all the leads on this investigation. And Bradley Poissant, Jason's friend, was one of those leads.

Conner adjusted his wipers again. "It's snowing a lot harder than when we left the house. We better not waste time here or we might not make it back home." His four-wheel-drive truck was good in snow, but even it had limitations, especially in snow that was coming down at a clip of three inches per hour. "The house is right here."

A quaint yellow house came into view. It had a wide porch now coated with a fresh layer of snow. Conner debated pulling up the driveway, then second guessed himself. The street plows had left a large pile of snow chunks at the end of the driveway that he'd never get through. Apparently the mayor didn't ask the crews to give him any special treatment. The mayor was a pretty stand-up guy, which was why checking in with his son when he wasn't home felt a little underhanded.

The tires brushed against the snow piled on the

side of the road. He pulled away from the curb to give Grace room to hop out.

Conner put the truck in Park and turned to her. "Okay, if you recognize him at all from the gas station, brush the back of my hand."

"I only saw his profile." She seemed to be searching her memory. "Let's do this. If I think it's him, I'll touch your hand."

"I'll do the talking. See where we get."

"Are you going to give me this same drill every time we talk to someone?" Grace smiled at him, and he couldn't resist smiling in return.

"Sorry, can't help myself."

Grace followed the path Conner created through the foot of snow. A two-foot drift was gathered alongside a car parked in the driveway. He reached back and took Grace's hand to steady her. "You good?"

She nodded and mumbled something that was muffled by the scarf wrapped across the bottom of her face.

The newly fallen snow made the house seem empty. Still. Maybe no one was home. That theory was quickly dismissed when a pounding sound came from inside, like someone racing down the stairs. Had Bradley seen them walking up the driveway?

Conner fisted his gloved hand and pounded on the door. A shadow slowed behind the smoky glass insert on the front door. "You expecting someone?" a female voice shouted from inside. Conner and Grace exchanged glances.

"Do we have the right house?" Grace whispered.

"Yes." Conner raised his eyebrows. Bradley was an only child. "Looks like while the parents are away, the kids will play."

"But it's a snow day."

"You grew up in Buffalo. A snow day means no school. It doesn't mean kids aren't going to find a way to hang out, especially if they live near each other."

Grace frowned. "Snow days were meant for curling up in bed with a good book."

"Different strokes, I suppose." He lifted his hand to knock again, and the door swung open. A young girl with long blond hair answered the door with a surprised look on her face.

"Is Bradley home?" Conner asked, holding the storm door open.

"Yeah, we're hanging out. Watching movies. Can I tell him who's here?" Score one for the teenager. She didn't allow a stranger into the house.

"Who's there?" Bradley appeared in the kitchen, visible at the end of the hallway. He wore sweatpants and a T-shirt with a few small holes in it. Recognition lit his face and he strode toward them. "Hey, Captain Gates, how are you?" An eyebrow twitched. "Is something wrong?"

The young man tried to look out the door beyond Conner and Grace. His attention slipped right past Grace.

Probably a good indicator that he didn't have it out for her.

"Hi, Bradley. Do you have a few minutes to talk?"

"Yeah, sure." Bradley stepped away from the door, giving them room to enter. He placed a hand on the young woman's shoulder. "This is my girlfriend, Suze."

"Nice to meet you," Conner said. "I'm Captain Gates, a friend of the family. And this is a friend of mine, Miss Miller."

"Nice to meet you, too," Suze said, smiling warmly at Grace.

"Have you met Miss Miller?" Conner asked Bradley, scrutinizing the young man's reaction.

Bradley's mouth grew pinched. "I don't think so." He offered his hand and Grace took it. She didn't seem to be registering any concern that she recognized him from the hit-and-run at the gas station.

Suze pointed at Conner casually. "You're the officer that's related to Jason Klein. I remember you from the bonfire."

Conner tapped his fingers on his thigh. "Jason was my cousin's son."

"Real sorry about his death. He was a nice kid."

"Thank you. Suze, were you also at the party the night Jason died?"

"No." She shook her head for emphasis. "My parents wouldn't let me go."

Good parents.

"Bradley was there." She linked hands with her boyfriend and rested her head on his shoulder. "He feels so bad. Right, Bradley?"

"Yeah, if I had known he was wasted, I would have stopped him from driving."

"You didn't see Jason drinking a lot the night of the accident? Or taking pills?"

"Everyone was drinking. Some were taking drugs. I avoid that stuff." Bradley dragged his toe along the seam between two oak floorboards.

"Did you guys want to come in?" Suze asked, her gaze drifting from the visitors to her boyfriend and back.

"We're not going to stay long. It's really coming down out there. I just wanted to get a few more details straight about the night of Jason's accident."

"I told you everything already." Bradley scrubbed his hand across his face.

"I need some clarification. I've heard recent stories that Jason wasn't much of a drinker, and that he definitely didn't do drugs. In hindsight, him being *wasted* doesn't make a lot of sense."

"We all make mistakes." Bradley held out his free hand toward Conner. "Like that night at the bonfire. Boy, was I stupid." Bradley put on what Conner suspected was his best oh-golly tone. Why hadn't Conner noticed it before? "I'm happy to put the partying phase behind me."

"I hear you were on a college visit yesterday. Have you decided where you're going?"

If Conner hadn't glanced down at that exact moment, he might have missed Bradley giving his girlfriend's hand a quick squeeze.

What's that all about?

"I haven't made a decision. Not yet, anyway."

"It's a big decision. I'm sure you'll make the right one." Conner unzipped his jacket. "I have a theory, and I wanted your take on it."

"Oh yeah?" Bradley jutted out his lower lip and blew his bangs from his forehead.

"Since I heard rumblings that Jason hadn't been drinking, what if someone spiked his drink the night he died?"

"That's your theory?" Bradley frowned, giving it some thought. "That might explain why he was messed up."

"You know anything about it?"

Bradley's eyes grew round, as if he were shocked. Conner quickly held up his hands to reassure the young man. "I'm not suggesting you had anything to do with it. But perhaps you've heard talk."

"No way. I can't believe someone would do that."

"It's hard to believe," Conner agreed. "Well, if you hear anything, you know where to reach me."

"Sure do." Bradley dropped his girlfriend's hand, crossed his arms and smiled tightly.

"We'll see ourselves out." Conner opened the door and Grace slipped in front of him.

Bradley retreated into the kitchen while Suze was too polite not to see them out. Just before they stepped outside, Suze asked in a hushed voice, "Did they ever find out what Jason was on the night he died?"

Conner debated giving her a straight answer. "Yeah, he had a mixture of prescription drugs in his system." He listed a few of the brand names. "Do you know anything about that?"

"No," Suze said a bit too emphatically. The rims of her eyes grew red. "I was curious, that's all."

"Okay, then," Conner said. "Have a good day. Stay warm."

Grace paused and reached into her pocket. She smiled at Suze. "I'm writing a story on how the Amish and local teens hang out with each other despite their very different lifestyles. If you'd like to be part of it, let me know." She pressed her business card into her hand. Suze seemed confused, but took the card and slipped it into her back pocket before closing the door.

Conner and Grace bowed their heads, bracing against the wind. When they were back inside the truck, Grace turned to Conner. "Did you see that? Suze looked concerned. Like maybe she wanted to say something more, but couldn't."

"I thought the same thing. Smart move on giving her your business card. Maybe she'll feel more comfortable calling you rather than the sheriff's department. Less threatening, maybe."

Grace plucked off her gloves. "Do you think we should have pressed her more before we left?"

Conner shook his head. "If she talks, it'll be when Bradley's out of earshot." He started the engine and turned on the wipers. The blades swept off the light dusting of snow. "We'll have to wait and see if our little visit pays off."

Retired sheriff Harry Gates lifted the glass coffee pot out of the automatic coffee maker and set out two mugs. Grace drew in a deep breath, the smell of strong coffee filling her senses. Despite not being much of a coffee girl, Grace felt nostalgic when it came to the scent. Her dad had been a big coffee drinker.

"Have a seat." Harry carried the two mugs over to the small table next to a window overlooking the driveway. "Nice of you guys to stop by. It's really blowing out there." Outside the window, Conner had powered up the snowblower and was slicing a path down the driveway, the snow shooting up in an arc and the wind blowing it back into Conner's face. Grace shuddered.

"Not much of a hardship for me." Smiling, she lifted the mug to her lips and took a small sip. "I'm sitting in the cozy, warm kitchen with you."

"My pleasure." Harry smiled. "Have you made any progress in your investigation?"

"Which one?" Grace tried to read the older gentleman to determine if he was still upset she was a writer, considering the trouble he'd had with the reporter from the *Quail Hollow Gazette.*

"Ah, you couldn't resist following up on both stories. Any new leads?"

"A few things. But it's been tough. I'm persona non grata around here."

"I may be retired, but I still hear things." Harry set his spoon down, and a brown stain spread across the napkin. "Regardless of my feelings for reporters, there's no excuse for what's been happening to you. Are you okay?"

"I'm fine. I think someone is trying to scare me away." She bit her tongue before saying more. She imagined the retired sheriff was also friends with the mayor.

"Did you ever ask yourself why they're trying to scare you?"

Grace angled her head in confusion. "Because I'm looking into the night of Jason's death, and someone doesn't want me to find out what really happened."

Harry lifted his mug to his lips and took a long sip. Above the mug, his eyes drifted to the weather outside. He seemed lost in thought. "That's one reason." He put the mug down and redirected his gaze toward her. "You're an easier target than, say, someone in law enforcement. However, either way, they're only attracting more attention to themselves."

"Criminals aren't always rational thinkers." She and Conner had had a similar conversation.

"True." Harry scratched the top of his head. "It seems they want to stop you before you uncover the truth. How many years has it been since your mother's murder? That's a deeply buried secret. I wonder if maybe you've stumbled upon something in your mother's case?"

If she had found something of value in that case, it had eluded her. "I believe I'm drawing attention because of Jason's death."

"I don't know."

"Really? What if the harassment is related to my mother's murder?" She studied the retired sheriff's face. "That would mean someone who was involved way back then is still around." Nerves tangled in her belly. "What's the likelihood?" She shook her head, the absurdity of the thought settling in. "No, it has to be related to the night Jason died."

Harry tapped the handle of his mug. "You're probably right. Kevin and I have been rehashing the case of late. We're still coming up blank." His eyes slanted in a thoughtful gesture, and Grace realized for the first time how much Conner resembled his father.

Grace took another sip of coffee, then set her mug down. "Nothing much to report. I did hear something strange, though." She took a deep breath, measuring her words, then smiled, feeling a little embarrassed to keep bringing up a nearly three-decades-old case. "When you were investigating my mother's death, did you uncover anything about former boyfriends?"

The retired sheriff's forehead furrowed. "Can't say that we did." He took another sip of coffee. "From what I gathered, your mother married your father when she was eighteen. I'm sure she had her usual running-around period. Most Amish do. By all accounts, she didn't waste time getting baptized and married to your father. No other Amish suspects came under our radar. Why? What did you hear?"

Grace's mouth went dry. She struggled to find her voice. Could she ask if her mother had considered leaving the Amish with an outsider? It felt too much like a betrayal of her mother's memory.

Grace ran her fingers across the edge of the table, realizing she was making this personal. This was a story and a good one at that.

But how can I not make this personal?

"I was wondering if someone who wasn't Amish showed a special interest in my mother."

Harry got a faraway look in his eyes. "Your mother was beautiful." A blush of pink infused his cheeks. "If you don't mind me saying so. However, I had never heard anything about her dating an *Englischer*." He rubbed a hand across his jaw, rough with stubble. "No one mentioned anything like that." He met her gaze. "If I were you, I wouldn't be wasting time on that theory. Your mother was a good Amish woman. No one ever said otherwise."

Grace nodded her agreement, unwilling to call into question her mother's character. That certainly wouldn't help the investigation.

Inwardly, Grace tried to shed the growing confusion that tracking this story had caused. Thinking she could do a story in Quail Hollow had been her first mistake. Believing she could be impartial had been her second.

"I haven't been able to find any real new information on my mother's murder. Maybe it was a silly idea to try to write a story on it. Perhaps I'll focus on the original story." She smiled. "But, happily, I got to know the Hershberger family. Maryann knew my mom."

"Maryann was quiet. It was hard to get any information out of the Amish. Your mother's death really impacted the community."

"They can be quiet." Grace dragged a hand through her hair. "The Hershberger family seems to be warming up to me. Maryann's daughter Emma is going to start working at the bed & breakfast."

"That's great." He leaned toward her. "I really like you, Grace. You might just change my opinion about your profession after all."

His comment caught Grace off guard and she laughed. "Was that almost a compliment?"

"Maybe it was. But I hope you remember that there are people behind your stories. Namely, Jason Klein and his grieving mother."

"I'll do my best to respect that." Her mind drifted to Conner's request that she hold off on posting updates online because of their impact on Jason's mom.

Harry smiled tightly as if he doubted that was possible.

Just then, Grace felt her cell phone vibrate in her sweater pocket. Something told her to check it.

"Excuse me a second," she said, pushing away from the table. "I should take this."

"Go for it."

Grace stepped into the family room and lifted the phone to her ear. "Hello?"

"Grace Miller?"

"Yes." Grace pressed the phone to her ear, fearing she'd miss what the caller was saying.

"This is Suze, Bradley's girlfriend."

"How are you?"

"Okay, um..." She was soft-spoken. "My grandmother's medication is missing. I didn't want to say anything until I went home to check."

A slow, steady beat thrummed through Grace's ears. "What kind of medication?"

"The kind found in Jason's system the night he died."

Grace shot a glance toward the kitchen. Harry seemed focused on Conner clearing the driveway. She turned back around and spoke quietly into the phone. "Would Bradley have had access to the drugs?"

"Yes, he used to joke that he could make a lot of money by selling them at school. I blew him off. I thought it was a stupid joke. Well, my grandma died last fall—"

"I'm very sorry."

"Thanks..." Suze sniffed. "I forgot all about it until earlier today when the deputy said something."

"Does Bradley know you checked your grandma's medication?"

"No! Shortly after you left, I told him I wasn't feeling well. I went home and checked my grandma's bathroom. She lived with us before she died. I know my mom hasn't gotten around to clearing anything out." Her voice shook. "Do you think Bradley drugged Jason? I can't imagine..."

"I don't know. I need you to do me a favor. Don't say anything to Bradley. Okay? Promise?"

"I promise."

"I'll talk to Captain Gates. He'll follow up."

"Okay." Suze sniffed again. "Did I do the right thing by calling? I don't want to get Bradley into trouble, but…if he did that to Jason…" Indecision, disgust and uncertainty dripped from her tone.

"You did the right thing. Now, don't say another word about it to anyone until you hear from Captain Gates."

Grace ended the call and stood motionless in the living room. Had Bradley stolen the prescription? They'd need proof.

Grace returned to the kitchen and detected a shift in Harry's posture. Staring out the window, he set down his coffee mug, and the brown contents sloshed over the edges. She drew closer to the window to see what had caught his attention. A car was parked in the road, and a man in a long black coat was charging up the driveway.

Plowing the snow, Conner seemed oblivious to the man approaching. He adjusted the chute on the snowblower, narrowly missing the man with the arc of white snow.

"Who is that?" Grace asked, staring intently.

"The mayor. And he doesn't look happy."

TWELVE

Hunkering down in the collar of his winter coat, Conner pushed the snowblower up his father's driveway. At the rate snow was falling, he'd have to swing by and clear the driveway again in a few hours. Conner hated to see his father out in the cold, even though he was more than capable of clearing it himself.

Who was he kidding? *He* hated to be out in the cold, too. Good thing he didn't mind putting his truck into four-wheel drive and zooming up his own driveway that rarely saw a shovel or a snowblower.

Conner reached the top of the driveway and cranked the chute to blow the snow to the far side of the driveway. He came up short when a black form charging toward him caught his attention. Adrenaline shot through his veins, making him forget about his frozen face, despite his winter hat tucked low on his head.

Conner shoved the snowblower into Neutral, then, when he realized it was the mayor, he turned it off. "How can I help you, Mayor?"

"I thought maybe you'd be here after stopping at my house."

"I'm helping my dad out."

"Listen, Conner, I'm real sorry about your cousin's son, but you have to stop bothering *my* son."

Conner tucked his gloved hands under his armpits. "I wanted to ask him a few questions about the night Jason died."

"Haven't we covered that ground more than once? The kid is wrecked." The mayor's nose had turned bright red, matching the tips of his ears. The guy needed a hat. "I want him to move on. Go to college. I don't need you to keep dragging him back to that night. The poor kid feels awful."

Something about his choice of words bothered Conner. "Why does he feel awful?"

The mayor fell back on his heels. "What do you mean? He lost his best friend. Of course he feels awful."

"How did you know I was at your house, anyway?"

"A neighbor recognized you. Said you were with some woman." As if sensing "the woman" was close, the mayor's eyes drifted to the house, then returned to him. "We need this whole situation to go away."

"Situation? Jason died. It's never going to go away." Conner's cheeks grew fiery hot, despite the polar wind whipping his face.

The mayor seemed to deflate a little, realizing what he had said. "I'm sorry. This whole situation—I mean, Jason's tragic death—has thrown everyone for a loop. Bradley is struggling. Really struggling. I'm worried about his mental health. I need for him to move on. I love my son. I don't want this to derail his life."

Conner bit back the argument that Jason didn't have the option to move on. Yet no one could fault the mayor for wanting only good for his son. Maybe that was the best thing. Besides, without any evidence, their theory was all conjecture at this point. Would they needlessly ruin another young life?

"I talked to the sheriff, and he said you're supposed to be on vacation."

Conner raised his eyebrows, but didn't say anything.

"Come in before you both freeze," Conner's father called from the front door, sounding very much like the authoritative sheriff he had once been. "Come in, both of you."

The mayor strode toward the door, traipsing over a few inches of fresh snow. Conner had just cleared that walkway. It was going to be a long day, for more than one reason.

Conner made sure the snowplow was off and

followed the mayor into his father's home. His father grabbed two mugs from the holder and proceeded to fill them up.

He handed one to the mayor and waited for Conner to take off his gloves before offering him the other.

Conner set the mug down, afraid the coffee would upset his already roiling gut. He yanked off his hat. Chunks of snow fell to his father's hardwood floor. He pulled his arms out of his heavy coat and tossed it over the chair.

"What brings you here in this weather, Mayor?" his father asked.

The mayor hesitated for a moment before answering. "Checking on why Conner and his friend here were at my house talking to my son."

"Like I said in the driveway, we were following up on some things, that's all."

The mayor set down his coffee mug forcefully. "I don't know why I came in. I don't have time for this. Thanks, Harry. We'll catch up at the diner one of these days."

"Sure," Harry said, taking a step toward the mayor. "You pick the time. I've got lots of it."

"Mayor?" Grace spoke up for the first time. "Everything I've heard about you leads me to believe you're a stand-up guy."

"Is there something you want?" The mayor lifted his chin, practically puffing out his chest. "I don't believe we've met."

Grace smiled and held out her hand. "Grace Miller. My sister Heather opened the bed & breakfast."

"Yes, yes…" He strolled toward her and held out his hand in the easy way of politicians. He pumped her hand twice before pausing and adding, "You were the woman at my house talking to my son?"

"I was. I'm working on a story about the night Jason died."

The mayor visibly flinched. "I was telling Conner that my son has taken Jason's death hard, and I'd appreciate it if you stopped asking questions. It's too painful for him."

"I can imagine." There was a coldness to Grace's words that struck Conner. She seemed to be calculating something. She met Conner's gaze, then looked at the mayor. "Would you give the sheriff's department permission to search your home for some prescription drugs?"

The mayor jerked his head back. "What are you talking about?"

Conner stared at Grace. Obviously something had transpired between the time he put his jacket on and went outside to clear his father's driveway and now. He wanted to take her to another room and talk privately, but something told him he had to let it play out. To trust her.

"I know you love your son. However, I think

he may have done something very stupid. Something that may have led to Jason's accident."

The mayor shook his head. "No way. You're wrong."

"Perhaps you'll allow Conner to call the sheriff's department. Allow someone to search the house, perhaps your son's room, for prescription drugs that don't belong to him."

The mayor crossed his arms. "Is that what it will take to make you both stop?" The mayor's gaze bounced from Grace to Conner.

Conner studied Grace for the briefest of moments before facing the mayor and nodding.

"Make the call then." The mayor reached for the door handle. "One condition—neither of you can be involved."

"That was a pretty gutsy move," Conner said, pacing back and forth in his father's kitchen. Once the mayor had left, Conner called Sheriff Flatt to conduct the search of the Poissant residence. His boss wasn't too thrilled on how things had unfolded, but he couldn't ignore Conner's request, especially since the mayor had given them permission.

"Perhaps I should have waited and discussed it with you first. If I had, Suze might have folded and told Bradley what she had done. I couldn't take that risk." Grace crossed her arms and leaned back in the kitchen chair. She shuddered as the wind pelted the glass.

"Time was critical here." Harry looked at Grace with something akin to approval. "The mayor and his family have been friends of mine for a long time. If their son drugged Jason—" he shook his head slowly "—that will be hard to forgive. But the kid needs to pay."

Conner smiled sympathetically at his dad and placed his hand on his arm. "Let's wait and see." Grace could tell Conner was still hoping Bradley was innocent in all this.

A sense of loss knotted Grace's stomach. She missed her dad. For years it had just been her and her sisters, and Grace had chosen to travel the world rather than connect with either of them. Of course, Heather's violent husband had had a hand in keeping her isolated.

Grace glanced at the clock on the wall. "How long do you think it'll be till we hear something regarding the search?"

"Not long."

A knock sounded on the door. "It's like Grand Central around here," Harry muttered as he shuffled to the door in his slippers. "Ah, Kevin." Harry's voice traveled from the front room to the kitchen where Grace was waiting with Conner.

"There's a lot of commotion at the mayor's house. Do you know what's going on?"

"Come on in." Harry led Kevin to the kitchen. "Want some coffee?"

"Um…" Kevin seemed to come up short when he noticed Grace.

"Hello," she said. "Quite a storm out there."

"Sure is." He unzipped his jacket and shrugged out of it. "Any chance you know what's going on at the mayor's house?" When no one answered right away, he added, "Aw, come on. You know I'll find out soon enough. I'm a retired undersheriff. Don't be such a stickler."

"Have a seat," Conner said, and he explained the situation. "Since it's only speculation at this time, please keep the information confidential."

"Of course," Kevin said, a million thoughts behind his bright eyes. "It's a shame when a decent guy like the mayor is saddled with a kid who thinks the world owes him everything."

"Why do you say it like that?" Grace asked.

"The kid has everything going for him, makes a few mistakes, stumbles, then decides to take down those around him. Shame." Kevin shook his head in a world-weary way.

"Let's wait and see if they uncover anything," Conner suggested.

Grace's phone chimed again, and she answered. Emma wanted to see if maybe she could start working next week, after the storm had passed. The young woman must have been eager to start her new job to call again. Grace ended the call and smiled at the three pairs of eyes staring at her. "Emma Hershberger is going to start work at the bed & breakfast."

"Hershberger..." Kevin seemed to roll the name around on his tongue. "Maryann Hershberger was a friend of your mom's. Any relation? A lot of these Amish have the same name."

"Emma is Maryann's daughter. I went to talk to Maryann about my mom."

Kevin nodded. "You don't leave any stone unturned."

"Not much else to do while I'm cooped up here." Her face immediately flushed, realizing she had probably offended everyone in the room.

Conner's phone rang. He swiped his finger across the display. "Captain Gates."

Grace studied Conner's face for any signs that prescription drugs had been found at the mayor's house. After a frustrating series of one-word answers that told her nothing, Conner said, "I need to be the one to tell Anna." A muscle worked in his jaw. "Thank you. I understand. Yes." Conner ended the call.

"They found two prescription bottles under Bradley's mattress. Two of the same drugs found in Jason's system." Conner relayed the information.

Grace grew light-headed.

"They had the name Elaine Jankowski on them."

"Suze's grandma?" she asked.

Conner slowly nodded. "Suze's grandma."

"Unbelievable," Harry said.

"How hard will it be to prove that Bradley drugged Jason?" Grace asked.

"Not hard at all. After one of the deputies found the bottles, Bradley cracked. He confessed to drugging his friend. He had no idea things would turn deadly." He met Grace's eyes. "Your theory was right. He wanted people to think Jason wasn't such a good kid after all."

Grace took no pride in being right. Not in this case. She slowly sat down, feeling oddly sorry for Bradley, but even more so for Jason and all the lives ruined because of the young man's reckless decision.

"Did he confess to ramming the car at the gas station?"

"He claims a friend of his did that. They wanted to stop you."

"Hmm…" Grace gave it some thought. "No wonder Bradley was falling apart. Every bad decision he made led to two more."

"He hasn't confessed to anything else," Conner said to Grace in a somber tone. She assumed he was talking about the incident in the library basement and the break-in at the bed & breakfast. "I'm sure once we track down his friend, all the pieces will fall into place."

"Did the sheriff give you the friend's name?"

Kevin asked. "Your dad and I still know a lot of the troublemakers in town."

Conner rubbed his jaw. "Some kid, last name Younge."

Kevin gave a knowing nod. "Must be Jimmy Younge. Comes from a long line of delinquents."

Grace wrapped her arms tightly around her middle. "Sounds like everything is unraveling. We caught a break when we ran into Suze at Bradley's house this morning. If not for her..." She let her words trail off.

"Sometimes that's how cases are solved. A matter of being in the right place at the right time," Kevin said.

"That's for sure," Harry added. With that, he turned his attention to the storm outside. "The snow doesn't show any signs of letting up."

"Let me finish the driveway, then get you home." Conner smiled at Grace while he reached for his jacket. "I'll hurry up. We don't want to get stranded."

THIRTEEN

The following evening, Grace stepped away from the table after snapping her laptop closed. She had spent most of the day working on her article about the events that had unfolded here over the past few days and weeks. The story was good. *Really* good. Now she had to wait for the right time to post it.

She rolled back her shoulders, easing out the kinks from hunching over her laptop for hours. It wasn't often the son of a mayor set in motion the tragic events that ruined lives and intensified the focus on an otherwise sleepy little town. She blinked her eyes, surprised to see that it was already dark outside. She really could get lost in her work.

Good thing she had declined Conner's offer for dinner. As much as she wanted to spend more time with him, she feared they were getting too close. A romantic relationship wasn't in her plans. They had already settled that.

Standing and stretching, she strolled over to the fridge. She was grateful for the leftovers. Conner's father had made a mean meatloaf last night and insisted she take some home. She could get used to the family and friendships in Quail Hollow, yet she still had no plans to stay. Her writing took her out into the world. Gave her financial freedom.

She dug her cell phone out of her purse when it dinged. It was her editor.

When are you going to get me that piece? Amish won't be hot forever. Followed by a clock emoji, as in, "Tick tock, your time is running out."

She smiled ruefully. She felt that way about a lot of things of late: time was running out.

Not in the mood to deal with her editor, she set her phone facedown on the counter. She ran her hand across her chin and stared at the plate rotating in the microwave. There was a bigger story here. Maybe a book.

Did she have what it took to write a book? It would take a long time, and she wouldn't make any money for a while.

She bent her arm over her head and tugged on her elbow with the opposite hand, savoring the muscle stretch. Her phone chimed—this time, a phone call.

She flipped over her phone. It was a local number. Maybe Conner was calling her from a different phone. She slid her finger across the display and pressed the speaker button.

"Hello?"

"Hello," came a shaky female voice. "Grace?"

"Yes, this is Grace." She moved the phone closer to her mouth and spoke louder, as if that would help her hear the caller better. "Who is this?"

"Em…ma." The single word wobbled over the line.

Grace's heart dropped. "What's wrong?"

"I had to run some errands, and a deputy pulled my wagon over."

Grace blinked rapidly, trying to process what was going on. She had heard the sheriff's department was cracking down on underage drinking parties and driving under the influence. But Emma surely hadn't done anything.

Grace didn't want to ask the question over the line when a deputy was probably standing right there, allowing Emma to use his phone.

"The deputy said he'd let me go home if someone came to pick me up."

"Okay, I'll be right there. Where are you?"

Emma gave her directions. She wasn't too far. Grace grabbed her coat and ran out the back door. With Bradley's arrest, they hadn't felt the need to station Becky at Grace's home again tonight.

Grace slowed down when she remembered

Zach's truck was buried after the heavy snowfall. It would take her forever to dig it out. She ran back in and dialed Conner's number. Maybe he could give her a ride. His phone went to voice-mail and she paused, then hung up without leaving a message.

A little voice in her head cautioned her. She couldn't keep calling on Conner when she needed something *and* push him away at the same time. She wasn't being fair to him.

Grace's gaze drifted to the bulletin board in the kitchen with a list of local services. She dialed the number and seemed satisfied that she had done the right thing when a short time later a white van pulled up along the bottom of her driveway. He probably didn't want to risk getting stuck in the snow.

Grace ran outside and hopped in. The driver explained that he had just dropped someone off nearby.

She said a silent prayer of gratitude. After everything that had gone wrong lately, she was thankful for a timely ride. She hated to leave Emma out in the cold for long.

Grace gave the driver directions. A short time later, snow and slush kicked up under the van's tires as the driver slowed and pulled over on the opposite side of the road from Emma's horse and wagon.

"Who pulls someone over in this weather?"

Grace muttered, not expecting the driver to answer. She released her seatbelt and leaned forward to study the pickup truck with a flashing dome light on its dash.

Strange, not a regular patrol car.

The deputy, his face obscured by the brim of his hat, stood next to the wagon. Emma was still sitting on the wagon's bench, wearing a heavy black bonnet and winter cape. Something didn't feel right. Grace grabbed the handle of the sliding door. "Wait here, please," she told the driver. "I shouldn't be long."

She hopped out, careful to avoid the patches of ice. The harsh wind slapped her in the face. Holding the collar of her coat tight at the neck, she crossed the road to where the officer stood with his back to her, talking to Emma.

"What's the concern here, deputy?" Grace said, both confused and angered by the situation. Her only restraint came from her gratitude that the deputy had allowed her young friend to call her. Emma wasn't a troublemaker or a drinker, not that Grace knew, anyway.

The officer turned around and Grace jerked her head back. "Kevin?"

"Hi, Grace. I understand you've come to rescue Emma."

"I'm confused. I thought you were retired."

Kevin rubbed his gloved hands together against the cold. "The sheriff hires some of us back on a contract basis to keep the streets safe. I'm sure you understand."

"Not exactly. In fact, I'm sure this must be a misunderstanding."

"*Yah*, I was careful," Emma said.

"You were weaving all over the road. I think you might have had too much to drink. I pulled you over for your own protection and that of anyone who might come into your path."

"Were you drinking?" Grace stared into the frightened Amish girl's watery eyes.

"*Neh*. I promise. I'm coming back from checking on my sister. She's expecting a baby."

"Is Ruthie okay?"

"*Yah*. I don't think the baby is ready to meet us." A small smile flickered on the young woman's sweet face.

Grace squeezed her hand and whispered, "Don't worry. I'll handle this and get you home."

"Thank you. I'm not sure my *mem* would be too happy if the sheriff's department brought me home."

"I understand." Grace let out a long frustrated huff and turned her attention to Kevin. "What do you do in situations like this? Obviously, you allowed her to call me. Can I promise you that I'll see her safely home?"

Kevin seemed to ponder this a minute. "She needs to be more careful. It's dangerous out here on the roads at night, especially for young ladies who've been drinking." The underlying meaning of his words sent fear skittering up Grace's spine: women, alone, night.

"I wasn't drinking," Emma insisted. Grace touched the young woman's arm, reassuring her. Kevin was going to let her off with a warning. No harm, no foul. It seemed pointless to argue.

"I can take you home, Emma. Let's go."

Emma started to scoot off the bench of the wagon when her eyes grew wide. "My horse. I can't leave her on the side of the road." Emma looked even more panic stricken now.

Grace glanced at Kevin. Surely they've run into this predicament before. "What do we do about the horse?"

"I can't allow you to drive." Kevin's tone lacked compassion.

"Please, I'm not…" Emma let her words trail off in exasperation.

Kevin turned to Grace. "Do you know how to handle a horse?"

Grace pressed a hand to her chest. "Are you kidding me?"

"Okay, I have an idea. You drive my truck—you can drive, right?—and I'll take the horse back to the barn at the bed & breakfast. It's closer than the Hershberger farm."

"Yes," Grace agreed, eager for a solution. "I can have Eli bring the horse and wagon to your home in the morning." She addressed the last part to Emma.

"Okay," Emma said, clearly not sure about any of this.

Grace walked Emma over to the van and pulled open the door. She could feel Kevin's eyes on them from across the road. A fluttering feeling settled in her belly. Grace leaned in close. She needed a plan. A backup in case something went wrong.

But you know Kevin. You're just cautious because of recent events. But…

Unable to shake her misgivings, Grace leaned in close to her Amish friend. "Emma, I should be home in thirty minutes. Once I get home, I'm going to call the business phone in your barn. If you don't hear from me by then, call 9-1-1 and ask to speak to Captain Conner Gates. Tell him exactly what happened. Tell him that Kevin Schrock was the man who pulled you over. Kevin," she emphasized. Grace considered jumping into the van with Emma and leaving the scene.

"I don't understand…" Emma started.

"What's going on?" Grace jumped when she realized Kevin was standing right behind her. He took her arm firmly, and she looked up at him with a question in her eyes.

He eased his grip a bit. "Come on. Let's get the horse safely home." Kevin grabbed the door handle and slammed it closed with Emma inside. He handed the driver some money through the open driver's side window, then tapped the roof of the van. "Safe travels." Then he turned to Grace. "Let's get this horse settled." Despite his innocuous words, a dark shadow lurked in the depths of his eyes.

"The driveway is plowed and the walks are shoveled." Conner took off his gloves and hat, then stomped his boots on the carpet just inside the entryway at his dad's house.

"I'm more than capable," his father hollered from his recliner in front of the TV toward the back of the house.

Conner walked through the dining room and took off his coat. He threw it over the chair "I know. But I don't mind."

His father laughed. "You don't even plow your own driveway."

Conner tilted his head. "Just gives me more time to do yours." He sat down on the edge of the couch in the adjacent family room.

"Actually I'm surprised. I thought you'd be trying to charm your lady friend before Heather and Zach get home from their honeymoon." Conner's father took a sip of his soda and leaned back in his recliner. "I don't imagine she'll be sticking around town much longer."

"Yeah, well, you know me. More the bachelor type." And she had refused his dinner invitation.

His father aimed the remote at the TV and turned the volume down. Setting his soda on the side table, he shifted in his chair to get a good look at his son. "I've never been one to speak from the heart. And my motto's always been live and let live, unless, of course, that involves going against the law."

"Not sure I'm following." He and his father discussed sports, weather, the occasional case. Not feelings.

"I have to say my piece. Up until now, you've dated here and there. I always bought into your claims that you preferred bachelorhood. The freedom of it all. I can see why you might think that's true." He held out his palm and plastered on an exaggerated smile, indicating his own living situation. "Sometimes I think you chose to be alone because of how your mom and I hurt you."

Conner held up his hands, not willing to get into this with his dad. Conner's mom had hurt both of them when she walked out after Sarah Miller's murder case took over his father's life. She claimed she could never compete with a dead woman for his father's attention. His father claimed his mother never understood the stresses of the job. At a standstill, they never reconciled.

"I know you had a job to do and Mom didn't understand. It's an important job. I get it."

"I don't think you do. Don't let this job consume you. If you can find happiness, grab it. Grace needs a guy like you. A good guy. Show her what a good guy is like."

Conner dragged a hand through his hair. "She's witnessed a lot in her lifetime. Losing her mom to violence. Knowing her former brother-in-law terrorized her sister. That shapes a person."

"You can change that. For both of you," his father pleaded.

Conner lifted a shoulder, unable to see how their very different lives would fit together. Starting to feel uncomfortable at all this touchy-feely talk, he asked, "Did you order the pizza?"

"Yep, should be ready."

Conner went to the front hall and pulled his father's coat off a hanger. "My coat's wet. I'm going to grab yours."

"No problem. Pick up more pop while you're out," his father hollered from his cozy spot in front of the TV.

"Sure thing." He stepped outside and the wind felt raw on his exposed head and hands. The key was to dress for the weather, only then could people embrace it.

Grace wasn't a fan of the cold weather. He

couldn't help but wonder if she could be convinced to make Quail Hollow her home.

Driving Kevin's truck, Grace pulled out behind Emma's wagon with Kevin behind the reins. He told her to follow him with her flashers on in his truck. Something about this seemed very wrong.

But would a man who bothered to care for a horse mean her any harm? Perhaps I'm overreacting.

She reached into her pocket and pulled out her phone. She didn't like to use her phone while driving, but figured this couldn't wait. She dialed Conner's number and held her breath. Her shoulders sagged when it went to voicemail again.

"Where are you?" she muttered.

"Leave a message..."

"Conner, it's me again. Listen, Emma Hershberger got pulled over by Kevin Schrock. He said he was working with the sheriff's department on a contract basis." She tried to keep her voice even. "Just seemed odd. I put Emma in a van home and right now I'm driving his truck back to the bed & breakfast behind him. He's driving Emma's wagon. Strange, right? I don't know." As she rambled on, she began to question why she called. "Just call me when you get this."

Grace ended the call and glanced at her phone's display. Who else could she call? She didn't want to call the sheriff's department because she didn't want Emma to get into more trouble if Grace's "bad feeling" turned out to be paranoia. What if they sent a deputy to Emma's house? Maryann would be upset. She slid the phone into her pocket and turned her full attention to the road.

Dear Lord, please keep me safe and quiet my racing thoughts.

Surprisingly, Kevin seemed comfortable behind the reins of the horse. It took longer to get back to the bed & breakfast than it had taken Grace to drive out. She didn't envy the Amish form of transportation in the bitter cold of winter.

Kevin stopped the wagon near the end of the driveway to the bed & breakfast. Grace pulled the truck in front of the horse. She gave Kevin a few minutes to unhitch the horse and guide it toward the barn.

She hopped out of the warm truck. Her instincts told her to go directly into the bed & breakfast, but she had to give Kevin his truck keys. She jogged over to the barn.

Grace waited in the doorway of the barn, stuffing her hands under her arms to keep them warm. "Looks like you're all set. Eli comes in the morning. I'll see that Emma's horse is fed and cared for until we can get her home. Here's your truck keys."

Kevin pushed the door of the stall closed and

patted the horse. "All set." He approached her and took the keys.

"Good night." She turned and picked up her pace toward the house, still unable to shake her nerves.

"Hold up." With heightened awareness, she tuned into Kevin's steady stride, fast approaching behind her. All her self-defense moves she never practiced floated to mind.

She knew she couldn't outrun him so she spun around and squared her shoulders. "Yes?" She hiked up her chin in a show of confidence she most certainly didn't feel.

"Would you like to go for coffee?" His expression was unreadable in the heavy shadows of the winter night.

Heat immediately pooled under the collar of her heavy coat. "No, thank you, I'm really tired." She turned again to walk toward the house. "Maybe another time," she quickly added, only to be polite.

Solid fingers latched on to her wrist, and Grace bit back a yelp. "No, you're coming now."

Conner returned to his father's house with the piping hot pizza. He set it on top of a hot pad on the dining room table. "Pizza's here."

Harry lowered the footrest on the recliner and stood. "Smells great." He gestured casually to

Conner's wet coat slung over the back of the dining room chair. "Your phone's been ringing."

"Oh, yeah?" Conner frowned.

Just as he slipped his hand into his coat pocket, the phone rang. He pulled it out and glanced at the display.

It was Dispatch. He slid his finger across the accept button. "Captain Gates."

"I have Emma Hershberger. She's anxious to talk to you."

He recognized the name. "Does she know I'm on vacation?"

"She insisted on talking to you."

Apprehension had Conner holding his breath. "Put her through."

"This is Emma Hershberger. Grace wanted me to call you." He pressed the phone closer to his ear, making sure he caught every word. "She wanted me to tell you that Kevin pulled me over. I promise, I wasn't drinking. The deputy let me call Grace to come pick me up."

Conner turned his back to the TV and walked toward the front of the house, focusing intently on the words spilling out of the young woman's mouth. "When Grace got there, the deputy let me leave with the hired driver while Grace and Kevin saw that my horse and wagon got safely back to her barn. She said to call you if she didn't call me in thirty minutes. I tried calling her myself but she didn't answer."

Conner listened to the long, winding tale. Not much of it made sense. One thing, however, stuck out: Grace had insisted this young lady call him. Grace must have sensed something was off.

"Did she say why she asked you to call me?" He turned and saw his father approaching out of the corner of his eye.

"She looked worried. I think she wanted you to know it was Kevin. She said make sure you tell him Kevin pulled me over."

"Where did you last see Grace?"

"On the side of the road with Kevin, the sheriff's officer."

"Is there a number where I can reach you, Emma?"

She rattled off the number and told him she had an answering machine in the barn and to leave a message if she didn't pick up.

Conner ended the call and noticed the missed calls from Grace. He listened to her message. She seemed concerned, but not overly. He tried to call her back. It rang a few times, then stopped. He hung up and dialed the sheriff's cell phone number. When he picked up, he asked, "Did you hire Kevin Schrock perhaps on a contract basis?"

"*Retired* Undersheriff Schrock? Um, no," the sheriff said. "I don't know what you're getting at."

"We might have a situation. I'll call you if I find anything out." He ended the call and explained to his father what Emma had told him. "Has Kevin ever pulled anyone over after he re- tired?"

"He's not allowed to. And you can go to jail for impersonating an officer."

He jammed one arm then the other into his damp coat sleeves. "Want to come with me? See what's going on?"

"Absolutely."

"Let's go." Conner swiped his keys from the table, tamping back his mounting fear. "Some- thing's not right."

Grace tried to yank her arm away from Kev- in's tightening grip, but he was stronger. "Please let me go," she said forcefully. "I called Conner from the truck. I'm expecting him any minute. He'll wonder where I am." She prayed a little white lie might derail whatever plans Kevin had. She had no idea why he was pulling her toward his truck.

"Your boyfriend won't make it here in time."

Her chest tightened and she tried to dig in her heels, but he was stronger. She pulled and wrig- gled and dropped like dead weight. She landed on her backside in the snow and scrambled back- ward. She'd have to get to her feet if she hoped to outrun Kevin.

"What are you doing?" he asked, his tone a mix of curiosity and disgust.

"I'm not going anywhere with you."

He stomped toward her punching holes in the snow with his boots "I thought you wanted to know what happened to your mother."

Grace wasn't going to take the bait. "Leave me alone. I'm not going with you."

His heavily shadowed face grew darker. "Now you sound just like her."

Grace's insides turned ice cold. She scrambled to her feet and debated if she could beat him to the house. "What do you mean, 'I sound just like her'?"

Kevin smirked. "Oh, don't get riled up. You know how much you look like her. It's only natural that you'd sound like her, too."

His words seeped into her brain. Her arms and legs trembled. There was more to their meaning than he was letting on.

Dear Lord, help me remain calm.

She doubted she could run to the door, unlock it and get in before he grabbed her. Perhaps she could keep him talking until Conner showed up.

If Conner showed up. She said a quick prayer that Emma called Conner as she had told her to. Or perhaps he had gotten her voicemail and decided to investigate.

Grace hiked her chin and tried to speak calmly. *Show no fear.* "Did you know my mother before she died?"

A slow smile tilted the corners of his lips. A

wicked glint lit his eyes in the moonlight. Sadness prickled the backs of her eyes. Her phone rang and a burst of hope rippled through her. She locked eyes with Kevin. Could she answer it before he stopped her?

Quickly, she reached into her pocket. Saw it was Conner. Frantic, she tried to accept the call, but Kevin slapped the phone out of her hand. "Not so fast. No more games."

Her phone sliced through the snow and disappeared. Her one source of communication was lost. A link to survival.

Kevin Schrock, the retired undersheriff, grabbed her arms and pulled them behind her. He shoved her toward his truck. Knowing this was her last chance, however feeble, she screamed and it echoed off the snow and barren trees. She wanted to cry, knowing it wasn't likely anyone had heard.

Kevin cursed, lifted his fist and slammed it into her head. Grace's all-consuming fear turned to blackness.

FOURTEEN

"None of this makes sense," the retired sheriff said from the passenger seat of Conner's truck. "Kevin Schrock pulled a young Amish woman over? Why would he do that?"

"I don't know. Maybe it was some kind of misunderstanding. Grace asked Emma to call me if she didn't call her in thirty minutes. Now Grace isn't answering her phone. Emma was under the impression that they were going to take her horse and wagon to the barn at the bed & breakfast for safekeeping. Let's go there. Clear this up."

"What are you thinking?"

"Kevin was acting outside his authority to pull someone over." Conner swallowed hard. He considered the fact that Kevin wanted to get to Grace somehow. How did that play into all this? The puzzle pieces didn't quite fit. Kevin had been his dad's longtime friend and subordinate. This was out of character for the man who had worn a badge for most of his adult life.

"You're friends with Kevin. Anything unusual going on in his life?"

"As much as it might surprise you, us guys don't talk about our feelings much."

Conner scrubbed a hand across his face. Maybe he should try another angle. "What role did Kevin play in Sarah Miller's murder investigation?" Something niggled at the back of his brain. Despite not seeing how all this would play out, Conner was convinced he was on the right path.

"What does that have to do with anything?"

"Dad, answer the question." He pressed down on the accelerator and the truck's engine roared. He prayed he didn't hit any ice. He didn't want to fishtail and end up in a ditch. Not tonight.

"He was my right-hand man. Sarah's case nearly killed me. I could never get her daughters out of my mind. I won't lie—it got emotional for me, whereas Kevin could separate his job from his emotions. He kept me focused. Kept me from charging off in all sorts of directions where I would have been wasting time and resources. You need to have focus with investigations like these."

Conner slowed at an intersection, glanced both ways and then sped through. "Were there any leads on which you felt he redirected you?"

"What are you talking about? Are you suggesting Kevin purposely interfered with the case?"

Conner hadn't heard this hard-edged anger in his father's voice in a long time. He hated to be challenged.

Conner gripped the steering wheel tighter. "I'm throwing out ideas. Trying to keep myself focused. Otherwise I might go mad imagining why Grace isn't answering her cell phone. Why would Kevin pull over an Amish girl when he's no longer working for the sheriff's department? Can we play around with a few what-if scenarios?"

"Yes." His father's answer was clipped. "Kevin was convinced a vagrant passing through town killed Mrs. Miller. And it was our best lead. Once, I thought we even had the guy, until he produced a rock-solid alibi. The guy was in Buffalo, locked up in the county holding center the week Sarah was murdered. But then we got information on another stranger seen in town that week." He fisted his hands. "Never could track him down."

"Who got that lead? The one on the second stranger?" Conner asked, keeping his eyes on the road.

"I don't know." His father grew silent for a minute. "I'm pretty sure it was Kevin." His father muttered under his breath. "I can't..."

"I wonder if Kevin generated this lead because he was trying to redirect your focus."

"I can't imagine."

"Were there any leads you *didn't* pursue, perhaps on Kevin's insistence?"

"A rumor surfaced that Sarah Miller may have dated an *Englischer*. We quickly put that to bed. It was hard enough for the family. We didn't want to drag Sarah's reputation through the mud."

He considered the exchange between Maryann Hershberger and Grace. Maryann claimed her friend had had an *Englisch* suitor. "What did Kevin think about that theory?"

"Not a lot. We were on the same page. No sense hurting the family more with baseless allegations."

Conner slowed and turned into the snow-packed driveway of the bed & breakfast. A wagon sat at the end of the driveway. "Looks like they made it here."

Conner and his dad hopped out of the truck at the same time. Conner ran to the back door and pounded on it. He canvassed the trampled snow while they waited. Either a few kids had been playing out here, or someone had had a struggle.

His father checked the barn and the two men met back in the center of the snowy yard. "There are two horses in the barn."

"The bed & breakfast only has one horse." Conner glanced around and noticed the tracks in the snow. "Looks like they brought Emma's horse and wagon here like she said. But there's no sign of Grace or Kevin."

The retired sheriff studied him with watchful eyes. "What's going on?"

Conner shook his head. "I wish I knew." He jerked his head toward his dad. "Call Kevin. Don't let on that we're looking for him. See what he says."

His father gave him a quick nod and opened his old-school flip phone. Conner paced outside the barn. Puffs of white vapor floated out from his mouth and disappeared into the black of night.

His father snapped the phone shut. "No answer."

"I'll try Grace again." He dialed her number. From across the yard, he heard a chirping noise. He followed the sound, made easier by the glowing light under a layer of snow.

He ran over to it, his boots crunching on the snow. Holding his breath, he bent over, stuck his hand in the snow and grabbed the phone. The screen displayed his name and number.

"Wherever Grace went, she left in a hurry," his dad said.

"How far does Kevin live from here?"

"He doesn't live far from the sheriff's department." The two men's eyes locked. Conner knew exactly what his father was thinking. "I'll call it in. Have someone go by and check his house. They'll get there before we possibly can."

The throbbing in Grace's head was the first thing she tuned into as she regained consciousness. The second was the stale smell of something closed up for far too long. The third was the set of events leading up to the pounding headache.

Fighting to keep her breath even so Kevin might think she was still sleeping, she opened her eyes a fraction. She had no idea where she was or the time. The room was dark, and a thin line of light seeped in under the door. The sharp springs of a cot poked her back.

She couldn't see much of anything. She held her breath and avoided any conspicuous movements. She didn't sense Kevin in the room with her.

She dared to open her eyes wide and study her surroundings. The heavily shadowed room came into focus. The thick drapes over the windows masked the time of day. She was in a room—a cabin decorated hunter chic—and the exit was about twenty feet away.

Dear Lord, help me get out of here.

Flattening her hand on the cot, she pushed herself up to a seated position and the springs groaned. Her aching head joined the protest. The room spun and what little was in her stomach threatened to make a second appearance. She lifted a hand to her aching head and was surprised to feel something. A prayer *kapp*? A bonnet. Blinking away her confusion, she touched the fabric gathered around her legs. A dress.

Head swimming, she pushed to her feet and crossed to a dresser and turned on a dim light. A full-length mirror sat in the corner. Someone had pulled her hair into a bun, placed on a bonnet and dressed her in Amish clothing. Frantic, she lifted up the hem of the gown and saw her jeans. The cuffs of her shirt poked up from the sleeves of the Amish dress. Someone had dressed her over her regular street clothes. She took small comfort in that, even as an underlying dread pulsed ever stronger through her veins.

Whoever had done this was sick.

Fearing Kevin had become unhinged, she knew she had to get out of there. As she quickly scanned the room, her thoughts grew scattered, and her face felt heated. If she hoped to make a break for it, she'd have to find her shoes and coat. Without them, she'd escape only to be found frozen to death in the harsh elements. She didn't see them anywhere.

A rustling sounded at the door. She grew rigid with indecision, uncertain if she should get back into bed and pretend she was still unconscious, or charge the door.

Her mouth went dry as the door swung open.

* * *

"Stay on the line with the deputy," Conner said to his dad. "Tell him we're headed to Kevin Schrock's house now. We're twelve minutes out. If he's there, make sure to keep him in sight. We're looking for Grace Miller. We can't risk him getting desperate."

His father nodded in the passenger seat, his phone pressed to his ear. He relayed the information. Conner could see the old fire in his dad's eyes. Conner hoped they'd find Grace safe and sound.

The thought of losing Grace forever forced all his true feelings to the surface. He had tried to stuff them down to be effective at his job. And because he knew she wasn't going to stay in Quail Hollow, anyway. That made it easy to pretend he didn't feel what he felt for her.

But the thought of losing her forever...

Hadn't his dad's inability to separate his feelings been his downfall? Or had his right-hand man purposely derailed the investigation?

A fist knotted his stomach as the pieces of the case started to click together.

As Conner raced toward Kevin's house and his dad waited on the phone, Conner asked, "Do you think Kevin was capable of hurting Sarah?"

His father stared straight ahead. "He was my friend. We don't even know that Kevin has Grace." His square jaw was set in determination.

"If he does, do you think he'd hurt Grace?"

His father sighed heavily, as if finally resigned to the fact Kevin wasn't who he thought he was. "I don't know anymore. I'm going to have to question everything I knew about Kevin. *If* he's involved." His dad straightened in his seat and turned his attention back to the person on the other end of the phone. "Yeah… You sure?… Okay." He ran a hand across his jaw. "Keep us posted."

His father flipped the phone closed. "No sign of Kevin at his house."

Conner eased off the gas, annoyance coursing through him. "Did they put out an alert for his vehicle?"

"Yes."

Conner pounded the steering wheel. The vehicle emitted a wimpy honk when his fist unintentionally made contact with the horn. An idea zipped through his mind. "Does Kevin have other friends, places he might go if he's desperate? If he needed someplace to hole up?"

His father bolted upright in his seat. "He's got an old hunting cabin. Goes there to clear his head. He brought me up there once a long time ago."

Conner's adrenaline spiked, and he had to consciously will himself to calm down. "Do you think you could find it now?"

"Yes!" His father's voice vibrated with excitement. "Turn left at the next intersection. It's about thirty minutes away."

FIFTEEN

"You're awake." Kevin stood with an armload of firewood. His demeanor was that of someone who had simply returned from a quick errand, not of someone who had kidnapped a woman and dressed her in Amish clothing.

"I'm awake," she replied, studying him carefully. "What are we doing here?" She tried to keep her tone even, nonaccusatory.

"I'm lighting a fire. It gets cold in here." He stretched out a hand and flipped on the light switch. "This provides better light than that old lamp." He dragged one hand over a piece of dusty furniture. "This place could use a good cleaning. I haven't been up here as much as I'd like."

Grace nodded slowly and winced. The pain ricocheted around her aching head. Kevin unloaded the firewood in the stand next to the fireplace in what seemed to be the master bedroom, yet he had set her up on a cot and not the bed that took up half of one wall. He rushed over to her like a doting boyfriend. "Does it hurt?" He studied her face in a way that made her skin crawl. He cupped her cheek, and she could feel gritty pieces of wood and dirt on his fingers. "I didn't mean to hurt you, but you were making such a fuss."

Grace leaned back a fraction and lifted her chin in a show of strength. "I need you to take me home now, Kevin. People will be looking for me."

He studied her face with an intensity that made her eyelid twitch. "You're not going home, Sarah. It'll be different this time."

Cold dread pumped through her veins. She knew it, even before he called her by the wrong name. Her mother's name. His link with reality had shattered to the point where Kevin thought she was a woman he had likely killed almost thirty years ago.

The walls closed in on her.

Kevin Schrock had been her mother's *Englisch* suitor. And when she rejected him he had ended her life.

It was the only thing that made sense.

"I never, *ever* meant to hurt you." Kevin narrowed his gaze, lost in thought. Lost in another time. Lost in the face of another woman. "We could have been happy if you had chosen me. You were too stubborn, self-righteous." A vein bulged on his forehead, and Grace knew she had to put on a performance.

She smoothed the tips of her trembling fingers across his forehead. She swallowed her revulsion. "It's okay. I'm here now."

Kevin let out a shaky breath and seemed to relax his shoulders. He even closed his eyes for the briefest of moments. "You are, aren't you?" He stared into her eyes, and it was all Grace could do not to blink. Not to cry. Not to lash out at this man who had killed her mother.

Dear Lord, help me.

"Why don't you light the fire?" She made an exaggerated show of shuddering to emphasize how cold she was.

Kevin searched her face for a long moment, then ran his hand down her arm. "Okay, honey. Stay here. I'll take care of it."

She nodded slowly, wishing her head would stop throbbing.

He took a piece of newspaper from the stack near the fireplace and crumpled it up for kindling. Grace's mind raced. How could she get out of here? She still had no jacket or shoes. How far could she get in the snow?

While her mother's murderer built the fire, he muttered something about taking care of the horse this time because people seemed more concerned about the horse than they had about

a murdered woman. People didn't always have
their priorities straight.

Grace had read about her mother's horse
being found wandering Quail Hollow after she
had been killed. She quickly shoved the thought
aside, determined to remain strong and focused
if she hoped to survive.

Grace took a chance and stepped toward the
bedroom door. Kevin froze like an animal sensing a shift in the environment. He pivoted on the
balls of his feet and slowly rose, a dark cloud
floating behind his eyes. "What are you doing?"

With her pulse thrumming in her ears, Grace
swallowed hard and forced a smile, fearing
Kevin would notice the twitch in her cheeks. "I
thought maybe I'd make us tea." Her eyes wandered toward the bedroom door. Maybe she'd
find a weapon in the kitchen.

Kevin considered her suggestion for a moment
before telling her to sit on the cot. He was the
host. He'd make the tea.

"Okay." She slowly sat down and clutched her
hands in her lap. He flicked the lighter and a
flame caught the piece of newspaper under the
firewood.

Kevin rubbed his hands together. "We should
have a roaring fire before long. It's a good thing
I came along when you were stuck on the side
of the road."

What?

Grace pressed her lips together, determined not to contradict him. Her nerves hummed as she plotted her escape. The longer he was in the cabin, the calmer he became. Maybe he'd eventually let down his guard. Until then, what would she endure? She wanted to ask him so many questions about her mom, about the recent attacks and break-ins, and how Bradley and his confession fit in. But she feared his precarious grasp on reality would further shatter and put her in imminent danger. He thought he was her rescuer. He was blending events...from tonight? And from almost thirty years ago?

"Are you warm?" he asked, coming to sit next to her and taking her hand in his. She fought the urge to yank it away.

"Yes..." She purposely let the word hang out there, preying on his need to please her.

"What is it?"

Grace smiled, doing her best to act shy. "I'm embarrassed to tell you this. I'd like to use the bathroom."

Kevin blinked rapidly. Then all of a sudden he stood and grabbed her wrist, pulling her up with him. "It's back here." He strode toward a door in the corner of the room.

Grace stopped and stared at him. "I need privacy."

He watched her, his eyes dark and unreadable. It was like part of him was seeing Grace and not trusting her, and another part of him was seeing Sarah, the woman he had fallen in love with. Become obsessed with. She prayed he'd be fooled long enough to give her time alone in the bathroom.

"I'll give you five minutes. I'll be standing right outside the door. Don't lock it."

Grace smiled tightly. She had no idea if it even mattered.

She went inside the bathroom, and a wave of nausea nearly doubled her over when she realized there was no lock on the door. Panicking, she knew she'd have to move fast. A tall, narrow glass shelving unit sat in the corner on the same wall as the door. Working quickly, she removed the tissue box, an ornamental duck and a few rolls of toilet paper. Silently, she slanted it across the door, forming a diagonal. It wouldn't keep someone out for long, but it would certainly slow them down.

At least, she prayed it would.

Tearing off her bonnet and stepping out of the Amish dress, she crept toward the window. She stretched up, felt for a lock on top of the window and twisted it.

Panic sent gooseflesh racing across her skin.

She planted two hands on either side of the window and froze. She glanced over her shoulder. If this window made any noise, Kevin would come charging in.

"Everything okay in there?"

"Yes. I'd feel better if you weren't standing right outside the door."

She thought she heard a little chuckle.

She turned both taps, opening the faucet full blast. It would mask the sound, but it might make him suspicious.

Quickly, she planted her hands on both sides of the window again and shoved. A horrendous rumbling noise sent the window up. A cold blast of winter assaulted her face.

Thank You, God.

At that exact moment, the sound of glass shelves exploded behind her.

Bam. Bam. Bam.

Kevin was busting through the door.

Not wasting any time, she hoisted herself through the small opening, her hips getting caught on the narrow window. Wiggling fiercely, she finally pushed her midsection through to the other side.

Just as she was about to pull her legs free, solid fingers grasped her ankle and wrenched it.

Grace released a bloodcurdling scream.

"How much farther?" Conner's nerves hummed in constant rhythm with the winter tires on the country road.

"Up here." His father leaned forward against his shoulder harness, searching for a landmark visible only to him. Then he pointed frantically toward a narrow break between the trees. "There! There! That road leads to his cabin."

Conner slammed on the brakes, threw it in Reverse and narrowed his gaze. "Here? The path between the trees?"

"Yeah, yeah, turn here. That sign is familiar." Sure enough, the headlights flashed on a sign with the words No Trespassing and the silhouette of a growling dog underneath.

Conner engaged the four-wheel drive and turned onto the small path. A single set of tire tracks told them someone had been down this way recently. "I would have never found this in a million years, Dad. Thank you."

"Don't thank me yet," his dad said, his voice somber. "Let's go rescue Sarah's daughter."

Conner pressed his foot on the accelerator, realizing for the first time that finding Grace safe meant more to his father than he had realized. It was his justice for Sarah.

"Dad, you can't blame yourself."

"I should have known. I never suspected Kevin. After me, he was closest to the case and probably used misdirection every chance he got." His father muttered something under his breath that Conner didn't quite catch.

"He had a lot of people fooled." Conner navigated the truck through the snow under a canopy of trees.

"I was the sheriff. The buck stopped with me. I failed Sarah. I failed her family."

Conner carefully navigated the snowy road, knowing nothing he could say would convince his father otherwise.

"Are you going to be able to drive all the way to the cabin?"

"Looks like Kevin's truck made it."

"It's not that much farther."

The rocking and slipping on the snow-covered road slowed their progress. As they rounded a curve in the road, a cabin with lights glowing could be seen set back among the trees.

"That's it," his father said, excited. "Right there. There's his cabin."

Conner stopped, cut off his engine and manually shut off the lights. "I don't see Kevin's truck, but someone's definitely there." He turned to his father. "You okay to walk from here? Gives us the element of surprise."

His father playfully patted his son's thigh. "This ain't my first rodeo." He zipped his jacket all the way up and put on his winter hat. "Let's go." Without waiting for a response, the retired sheriff pushed open the door. Conner slipped out of the vehicle. They both closed their doors at the same time with a quiet click.

They met at the front of the truck. "Snow's pretty deep," Conner said. "Let's follow the tire tracks until we get about fifty feet from the cabin. Then you go right, and I'll go left around to the back. Assess the situation."

Conner's gut tightened at the thought of what might be happening to Grace at this very moment. He found himself saying a quick prayer. He hadn't done that since his mom took him to church when he was a little kid.

His father nodded, and they both set off. The sound of their breathing was punctuated by the squeaking of their boots in the snow.

As Conner broke left, a scream pierced the night.

His blood ran cold.

Grace.

Conner took off running at the sound of her scream, his legs and arms pumping as he struggled through the deep snow. He turned the corner. Light—and Grace—spilled out of a window. Grace had her hands propped on the snow and was flailing. Kevin had his head and one shoulder out the window, and he had a firm grasp on Grace's ankle, after what was obviously a failed escape attempt.

"Let her go," Conner ordered.

"Get out of here!" Kevin growled, not taking his eyes off Grace.

"You're in a tight spot there. There's nowhere to go. Let her go," Conner repeated as he pulled out his gun.

Kevin shifted, revealing the gun he was barely

able to squeeze out on the other side of his body. "I may not be able to get you, son, but I have a clear shot at Sarah here."

"Her name is Grace," Conner enunciated slowly, trying to break through whatever alternate universe Kevin was in. Conner directed the beam of his flashlight at Kevin's face.

Kevin blinked a few times, anger sparking in his eyes. "She was supposed to marry me and get out of this awful town. If she couldn't love me, she wasn't going to have anyone."

Kevin began to sob. Conner crept closer.

Suddenly Kevin released his grip on Grace's ankle and crumbled on the windowsill as if someone had cracked him from behind. The gun fell from his hand and disappeared in a tunnel of snow beneath the window.

From inside the bathroom, retired sheriff Harry Gates hadn't missed a beat. "I've got him." He yanked Kevin back through the opening.

"Everything under control?" Conner shouted.

"Yep, got this jerk in handcuffs. How's everyone out there?" his father hollered out the window, his focus on his prisoner.

Conner bent down and scooped up Grace. Her head fell against his chest. "Are you okay?"

She shuddered against him. "I am now."

"Let's get you home."

Thank You, God, for keeping her safe.

SIXTEEN

Grace tried not to giggle as Conner touched the ticklish spot around her ankle, inspecting where Kevin had grabbed her and twisted in an attempt to keep her under his control. She leaned back in the rocking chair by the wood-burning stove in her sister's bed & breakfast and tried to think of serious things to stop her silly giggling, which wasn't too hard.

Her gaze drifted to the stairs where Becky had disappeared only moments ago. "Do you really think it's necessary to make Becky stay?"

"Hey!" Becky called from the upstairs landing. "You're going to give a girl a complex."

"Sorry," Grace called back, "no offense meant. Just hate to waste your time. All the people that have had it in for me are in custody. Or am I missing something?"

Becky came down the steps. "You should be safe. Conner wants me to stay another night or two. He thought you'd like the company after everything that's happened."

"You don't mind, do you?" Conner asked. A tingle raced up her foot from where he was still holding it.

"I certainly don't mind the company." She smiled at Becky, trying to ignore the effect Conner was having on her.

"Listen, I stopped over at the Hershberger residence on my way over," Becky said. "Emma's relieved you're okay."

"Did you explain to her mom that she didn't do anything wrong? I'd hate for her to get in trouble with her community."

Becky waved her hand. "Yes, she's fine. Their family wishes you a speedy recovery. Emma said she'll stop by in a few days. See about helping you around here."

"Sounds good."

Becky pointed toward the kitchen. "Mind if I grab some tea and head upstairs? I have a good book waiting for me."

"Sure thing," Grace said.

"And I'll make sure the alarm is set." Conner patted Grace's foot, gently placed it on the rocker next to him and stood.

Grace groaned. "What more could go wrong? You already have Bradley in custody for drugging Jason, and obviously Kevin's not going anywhere. That pretty much covers all the stories

I was digging into here in Quail Hollow." She crossed her arms and settled back in her chair. "I promise."

Conner studied her with an intensity that made her toes curl. "You're not going to ruin Becky's evening. I think she enjoys getting away at the bed & breakfast."

"She's good company. I don't mind. I appreciate her taking the time."

Conner brushed his hand across her shoulder, seeming hesitant to leave. Grace understood. They had been through a lot together. "Things will be wrapped up soon."

Despite Kevin's break with reality, he did have the wherewithal to tell his side of the story. He had hired some guy to knock the shelves over in the basement of the library to scare Grace away from her mother's story. He was rightfully afraid of what she'd uncover. A deputy had been sent to pick up the guy he'd hired.

"What about the person who rammed my car in the parking lot?"

"One of Bradley's teammates wanted to protect his friend. Misguided loyalty. He felt the team had suffered enough by missing the play-offs. He didn't want Bradley getting in trouble for spiking his friend's drink, too." Conner bowed his head and rubbed the back of his neck. "I fear for the next generation if they think hurting someone else is a form of loyalty."

"They're not representative of our youth. There are a lot of wonderful people in this world. I've met them while covering different stories. I have faith we're on the right track." She rubbed her arms absentmindedly.

He leaned over and picked up her foot from the rocking chair, sat down and rested her foot on his knee. "I admire that about you. You have faith despite all the horrible things you've experienced."

"My faith is the one thing that keeps me going."

Conner studied her foot while massaging it. He seemed hesitant, as if he was trying to figure out how to tell her something. He lifted his eyes to hers. "I found myself praying that I'd be able to save you. I haven't done that in a long time."

Grace reached forward and covered his hands with hers. "Thank you for being there for me."

"I wouldn't have had it any other way."

He set her foot down, then leaned in to brush a soft kiss across her lips. "You sure know how to have a quiet vacation in Quail Hollow."

"This was never meant to be a vacation. I came here initially to recover from an appendectomy." Her hand went to her side. "That seems so long ago."

"I'd hate to see what kind of trouble you could have gotten into if you hadn't been sick."

Grace cupped his cheek and ran her thumb

across the stubble on his jaw. "Well, thankfully, I'm fully recovered."

"Thank goodness." Conner took her hand from his face and kissed it. "You're okay? Kevin didn't hurt you?"

"Just a few bumps and bruises."

A hint of a smile danced in his eyes.

"I'll be okay. I promise," she whispered. The air in the room grew charged with an energy of expectancy that made butterflies flit in her stomach.

"I didn't realize how much I cared for you until I thought I lost you." He held her hand. Warmth spread up her arm, and she pushed the blanket down from around her shoulders.

"Did I thank you for saving me?" She hated the nervous squeak in her voice.

"More than once." He sat up straight and dropped her hand, as if he had switched gears.

Grace scooted toward the edge of her rocking chair, causing it to dip forward. She reached out and covered his hand resting on the arm of his chair. "I care for you, too."

"I sense a *but* coming on."

"We lead different lives. Your home is here. Mine is wherever the story takes me." She knew that stuff was superficial. The only thing truly keeping her from committing was her fear of relationships after losing her mom and witnessing her sister's violent relationship. If her dad were still alive, he'd no doubt tell her he'd marry her mother all over again, in spite of her heartbreaking murder. And Conner was not anything like her sister's ex. She had been using her fear as an excuse. Until now, she had never met someone worth taking the risk. Worth pushing aside her worries.

All her thoughts were jumbled and the only words she found were yet another excuse. "This would never work."

"I guess you can't blame a guy for trying." Conner laughed, a mirthless sound. "You'll have a great story to tell about your adventures in Quail Hollow."

She gently rubbed the back of his hand. "More than that, I finally have answers. My sisters will have answers. And my mom will have justice."

"I'm glad. I'm sorry it took this long."

Grace stifled a yawn. Conner covered her hand with his, keeping it warm. "I'll let you go to bed." He started to rise, and she stood with him. He took the opportunity to cup her cheek and kiss her, slow and gentle. After a moment, he pulled away. "I'm really going to miss you."

She nodded, unable to swallow around the lump of emotion in her throat. Unable to find the words to tell him she cared for him. Deeply. Too much had happened to make any sweeping promises she might regret in the light of day.

When she didn't respond, he cleared his throat.

"Follow me to the back door and set the alarm after I go."

"I will."

"Oh, and I'll send someone over to plow the driveway. I don't want you to be snowed in."

"Thanks." They walked in silence and she saw him out, then set the alarm and waited for the sense of loss to pass.

The next morning, Grace headed downstairs after a dreamless sleep. Despite the things she had yet to face, she finally had peace. Her mother's murderer had been caught.

When she rounded the corner into the kitchen, she came up short. "Hey, Becky. I didn't expect you to still be here."

The young sheriff's deputy smiled. Sitting at the table, she lifted her book with one hand and her coffee with another. "You know how it is when you say you're going to read just one more page?"

Grace laughed. She was really growing to like this woman.

"Conner wanted me to let you know they arrested the young man Kevin hired to attack you in the basement of the library."

"What about whoever broke in here?"

"Kevin confessed to that. He said that you reminded him of Sarah. He wasn't really clear on how he got through the window here at the bed

& breakfast or how he unlocked it. I'm sure he learned tricks over the years as a sheriff's deputy. He said he wanted to get close to you. See if you had uncovered anything about Sarah Miller's murder." Becky spoke as if Sarah wasn't related to Grace. "He hadn't expected you to come downstairs that night. He ran off instead of confronting you."

Grace's stomach knotted at the thought of surprising Kevin in the middle of the night. "I'm lucky Boots notified me of his presence. I hate to think…"

"Speaking of Boots, I haven't seen the kitty around in a while." Becky furrowed her brow and glanced around.

"She took off. My sister says she comes and goes and not to worry."

"Not to worry. Sounds like a plan." Becky gave her a sympathetic smile. "You have to move on. There's no way to understand the thought process of someone who's mentally ill. It seems Kevin eventually became obsessed with you, much as he became obsessed with your mom." She placed her book facedown to mark the page and stood. "I'm really sorry you had to go through all that." Becky flipped over the book, folded a corner of the page and then closed it. "You can finish that story you've been writing."

"Yeah…" The weight of indecision pressed

heavily on Grace's chest. Maybe she was too close to the story to be objective.

Voices floated in from outside, and Grace leaned over to look out the back window. "Oh, wow, my sister and her husband are home. Already?" Had she been that preoccupied that she'd lost track of the days? She hadn't thought so.

Becky stood and set her mug in the sink. "Looks like my cue to leave." She slowed and touched Grace's arm. "Take care, okay?"

Grace nodded. "Thanks for everything." The two women exchanged a brief hug.

"You're welcome." Becky picked up her overnight bag from the floor and slung the strap over her shoulder. She greeted Heather and Zach as she slipped out the back door.

Heather appeared suntanned and well rested. And happy. She flicked her thumb toward the yard with a confused look on her face. "Booking overnight guests while we're gone?"

"Long story." Grace hugged her sister fiercely. "You guys are back early."

"A few days early," Zach said with a broad smile.

"Miss this place too much?" Grace asked, confused.

"I was feeling a little queasy on the boat. We caught an earlier flight home from one of the ports."

Grace studied her sister. Heather glanced at

her husband, then back at Grace. She placed a hand on her midsection. "I'm pregnant." She hunched up her shoulders and a smile crept up on her face. "Morning sickness." Her happiness was contagious.

Grace hugged her sister again, and a tear tracked down her cheek. "I'm thrilled for you." She reached out and playfully tapped Zach's cheek with the palm of her hand. "And you. You guys deserve all the best."

"So tell me," Heather said, as she sat down at the table. "How have things been around here?" She glanced around the bed & breakfast, her pride and joy. "Looks like you held down the fort. I hope your stay in Quail Hollow was uneventful."

"Why don't you and Zach get settled first? We'll talk later." Grace didn't want to throw a wet blanket over their happy homecoming by telling her sister about her car. Hopefully, the collision shop would have it repaired soon so that her sister wouldn't be inconvenienced.

Heather pushed to her feet. "Sounds good." Zach breezed past with the luggage, and Heather followed him upstairs.

Grace turned and stared out the window. A wicked wind sent the top layer of snow into a mini tornado. She shuddered and wrapped her arms around herself.

The sound of another vehicle made her glance

toward the driveway. Conner's patrol car. She had thought they said their goodbyes last night. A lightness sent butterflies fluttering in her chest. She hustled to the mudroom, threw on her coat and opened the door, not caring if she seemed too eager to see him.

Upon noticing her as he walked across the yard, he took off his hat and smiled. Her heart melted a little bit more. He reached the back porch in a few long strides. "Becky filled you in?"

"About the arrests? Is it really over?"

Conner nodded. "Everyone involved has been arrested."

"Good." She rolled up on the balls of her stocking feet in the doorway.

"I've been doing a lot of thinking. I hope *we're* not over."

Grace tilted her head. Emotion trapped the words in her throat. A harsh wind whipped up and blew the hair from her face.

Conner stepped closer. "I couldn't let last night be the end. I don't want to say goodbye."

Tears burned the backs of her eyes. She'd be lying if she claimed they were from the wicked winds. "Neither do I, but I couldn't find the right words last night." She met his gaze. "I've always been afraid to get hurt, but I've never met anyone like you."

Conner took her hand and stepped into the

mudroom and closed the door behind them. "I understand. I promised myself I'd never repeat the mistakes of my parents. That I'd somehow protect my heart if I never risked it." He reached up and cupped her cheek. "But after thinking I'd lost you last night to that lunatic, I realized I'd been foolish." He traced her jawline with his knuckle. "You're too special to let go because I made a promise to myself to remain a bachelor when I was young and naïve."

Her face grew warm, despite the cool touch of his hand. A smile tugged on the corners of her lips. "Looks like we both had time to reflect last night."

He ran his fingers through her hair. "These feelings had been growing for awhile. The events of last night jolted me into realizing I couldn't keep ignoring them. I was afraid you'd leave before I had a chance to talk to you in person."

Grace reached up and wrapped her fingers around his wrist. "But where do we go from here?"

"I have an idea." He stepped closer and pressed a kiss to her lips.

Grace tasted like good coffee and morning sunshine. Conner hadn't slept much last night after nearly losing Grace. Then, this morning, he had gotten a quick phone call from Zach when they landed. Conner couldn't risk Grace leaving without knowing how he truly felt.

He stepped back and Grace tenderly touched her lips. Dipping her head, she slipped past him and into the kitchen. "I imagine you have to get back to work? Can I get you a coffee to go?"

"That would be great." He watched her open and close the cabinets, probably looking for a to-go cup. Sensing her unease, he stepped up behind her and gently touched her back. "How about I stay for the coffee?"

"Oh, sure." She grabbed a mug, filled it and handed it to him.

He took a sip and decided to update Grace. Give her a minute to settle down, to process everything they shared. "This is great. Hey, I have good news about Katy Weaver. She went home from the hospital yesterday. The doctors feel she's on her way to a full recovery." The young Amish woman injured in the crash would get to live her life.

"What a relief."

"For everyone."

"How's Jason's mom? It had to be excruciating for her to know Bradley was responsible for Jason's death."

Conner nodded. "Having answers will go a long way toward providing her peace."

"I get it. I never thought we'd find my mother's

murderer." Grace's eyes brightened. "I can't thank your dad enough for leading you to the cabin."

"It brought my dad some measure of peace to know he didn't let down Sarah's daughter." He smiled.

"He didn't let down my mother either. That's on Kevin." Grace squeezed his hand.

Conner gestured with his coffee mug toward the interior of the house. "Your sister's home."

"They're upstairs unpacking." She smiled brightly and leaned toward him. "They came home a few days early because my sister was getting queasy on the ship." She lowered her voice. "They're expecting a baby!"

"That's great."

Grace met his gaze. "It looks like things are finally working out for the Miller girls."

Conner set his coffee mug down and took her chin gently between his fingers. "Things *are* working out. Remember that. Don't start second guessing things when I leave here."

She nodded.

"We have a lot of things to figure out, but we'll do that together." He covered her mouth with his. He pulled back a fraction and whispered, "I love you."

She tilted her head back and smiled. "I love you, too." She narrowed her gaze, then laughed. "Does that mean I have to move to the great white north?"

Conner raised his eyebrows. "Not if you don't want to. I could find a job somewhere else, as long as I'm with you. That's all that matters."

EPILOGUE

Six months later...

The early morning sun streamed into Grace's bedroom. She sat on the chaise lounge with her laptop, finishing up the reader letter to be inserted at the back of her book about life in the Amish community. She stopped typing, pressed her fist to her mouth and reread:

> My mother lived her entire life in the Amish community. I don't think ever in her wildest dreams could she have envisioned the lives her three daughters would go on to live after her untimely death. My memories of my mom are vague. But deep in my heart—despite the Amish caution against pride—I believe she would be proud of all of us.
>
> Proud that we persevered through difficult times.

Proud that we've found happiness despite all the sadness in the world.

Proud that we chose to live life with hope. And faith.

With a great sense of satisfaction, she closed the lid of the laptop. Grace was confident she had done everyone justice with this book with her thorough research. She had returned the articles to the library. She was pretty sure the librarian had forgiven her because she had been more than helpful with the follow-up research.

Setting the laptop aside, Grace stood and stretched out all the kinks from sitting too long. Perhaps she'd tweak the letter again later. Writing was rewriting, after all.

Opening the bedroom door, Grace stepped into the hallway of the bed & breakfast. Although Heather didn't expect her to, Grace had gotten into the habit of starting the coffee and putting out a few baked goods for the guests who were early risers. Emma would prepare a warm breakfast at nine o'clock sharp for the guests. She had taken over now full-time for her big sister now that Ruthie was the mother to a beautiful baby girl.

Heather and Zach had invited Grace to stay at the bed & breakfast while she wrote her book and planned her wedding to Conner. The least she could do was help out here and there.

After getting the coffee and baked goods set, Grace put on her sneakers and headed out for a run, another new habit. It was amazing how easily she'd adjusted to small-town life. It was far easier during the summer than the winter, but she was learning to take it all in stride. And Conner assured her theirs would be the type of relationship where she could travel the world to write her stories. He'd come with her when he could. Quail Hollow would be their home base. But more and more, she found contentment with writing longer features right here at home.

Home. After years of writing stories about other people, to give them a voice, it felt wonderful to have overcome her fears to find a voice of her own.

She paused at the end of the driveway and smiled when she saw Conner's truck pull up. They had gotten into a routine of jogging on weekend mornings when he didn't have to be at work.

He pulled over and hopped out of the truck. "Am I late?"

"No, you have perfect timing." She smiled up at him, and he leaned down and kissed her.

A light twinkled in his eyes. "Good morning."

"Let's get moving." Grace stretched her arms over her head.

"I still can't believe you've taken up jogging."

"I'm full of surprises." She jogged in place as Conner checked the laces on his running shoes.

"Do you think you'll take up skiing this winter?"

"One sport at a time, buddy." She shook her head and laughed.

"The key is to wear the right clothes."

"So I've heard," she said, sounding skeptical. "Hey, did you see? Zach put out the sign last night on the front lawn."

"I did." They both glanced over to the Conner Gates for Mayor sign.

"Are you having second thoughts?" she asked.

"I never have second thoughts. Are you?" he asked teasingly.

"About you running for mayor? That means I'll be the mayor's wife." She held up her chin proudly and gave him a regal smile. Bradley's father had resigned after all the negative publicity regarding his son. "Why would I have doubts about that? You'll make a great mayor. It wasn't exactly your plan. But plans change. You would have made a great sheriff, but that was before this opportunity presented itself."

"I'm excited about new possibilities." He paused. "But that's not what I meant." He planted his hands on her waist and pulled her toward him. "Our wedding is in less than two weeks. Are you getting cold feet?"

She leaned up and pressed a kiss to his lips.

"Absolutely not." She patted his chest. "I've never been more sure of anything in my life. Except that you're going to be the next mayor of Quail Hollow."

"Ah, from your lips to God's ears."

She cupped his face in her hands and smiled. God had certainly answered her prayers.

She gave him another quick peck and then spun around and started jogging toward the road. "Come on, slug. Try to catch me."

Grace didn't give Conner much of a chase. She laughed as she heard him approach from behind.

"Come on. You can run faster, can't you?" he asked.

Grace nudged his shoulder with hers. "I could, but why would I want to if it meant leaving you behind?"

* * * * *

*Look for the next Amish suspense book
from Alison Stone this spring.*

*And don't miss some of her previous
Amish books set in Western New York:*

*PLAIN PURSUIT
PLAIN PERIL
PLAIN THREATS
PLAIN PROTECTOR
PLAIN COVER-UP
PLAIN SANCTUARY*

*Available now from
Love Inspired Suspense!*

Dear Reader,

Welcome back to Quail Hollow, NY. This time we learned about Grace, sister of Heather from Plain Sanctuary. Grace had spent her life traveling, researching and writing about other people's lives. She avoided looking too deeply into her own life because it was too painful. However, when circumstances forced her to face her fears, she finally found answers, peace of mind and eventually happiness.

Have you ever avoided something only to discover that facing it head-on was the only way to walk through it? I know I have. This is when I'm reminded that I need to trust in God.

When I start writing a new series, like Quail Hollow, I have an idea where I'm going, but sometimes the creative process of writing leads me off in another direction. Deputy Becky Spoth walked onto the page in *Plain Jeopardy* to help keep Grace safe, and suddenly I knew she needed a story of her own. Please keep an eye out for Becky's story next from me with Harlequin Love Inspired Suspense.

If you'd like to keep up with my latest news and releases, sign up for my newsletter on my website at www.AlisonStone.com.

I can also be reached on Facebook under Author Alison Stone. You can also email me at

Alison@AlisonStone.com or write me the old-fashioned way: Alison Stone, PO Box 333, Buffalo NY 14051.

I enjoy hearing from you.

Live, love, laugh,
Alison Stone

Get 2 Free Books,

Plus 2 Free Gifts—

just for trying the Reader Service!

Get 2 Free Books,
Plus 2 Free Gifts—
just for trying the Reader Service!

YES! Please send me 2 FREE Harlequin® Heartwarming™ Larger-Print novels and my 2 FREE mystery gifts (gifts worth about $10 retail). After receiving them, if I don't wish to receive any more books, I can return the shipping statement marked "cancel." If I don't cancel, I will receive 4 brand-new larger-print novels every month and be billed just $5.49 per book in the U.S. or $6.24 per book in Canada. That's a savings of at least 19% off the cover price. It's quite a bargain! Shipping and handling is just 50¢ per book in the U.S. and 75¢ per book in Canada*. I understand that accepting the 2 free books and gifts places me under no obligation to buy anything. I can always return a shipment and cancel at any time. The free books and gifts are mine to keep no matter what I decide.

161/361 IDN GMWQ

Name _____ (PLEASE PRINT)

Address _____ Apt. #

City _____ State/Prov. _____ Zip/Postal Code

Signature (if under 18, a parent or guardian must sign)

Mail to the **Reader Service:**
IN U.S.A.: P.O. Box 1341, Buffalo, NY 14240-8531
IN CANADA: P.O. Box 603, Fort Erie, Ontario L2A 5X3

Want to try two free books from another line?
Call 1-800-873-8635 today or visit www.ReaderService.com.

*Terms and prices subject to change without notice. Prices do not include applicable taxes. Sales tax applicable in N.Y. Canadian residents will be charged applicable taxes. Offer not valid in Quebec. This offer is limited to one order per household. Books received may not be as shown. Not valid for current subscribers to Harlequin Heartwarming Larger-Print books. All orders subject to approval. Credit or debit balances in a customer's account(s) may be offset by any other outstanding balance owed by or to the customer. Please allow 4 to 6 weeks for delivery. Offer available while quantities last.

> **Your Privacy**—The Reader Service is committed to protecting your privacy. Our Privacy Policy is available online at www.ReaderService.com or upon request from the Reader Service.
>
> We make a portion of our mailing list available to reputable third parties that offer products we believe may interest you. If you prefer that we not exchange your name with third parties, or if you wish to clarify or modify your communication preferences, please visit us at www.ReaderService.com/consumerschoice or write to us at Reader Service Preference Service, P.O. Box 9062, Buffalo, NY 14240-9062. Include your complete name and address.

HWI7R2

Get 2 Free Books,
Plus 2 Free Gifts —
just for trying the Reader Service!

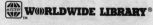

HOME on the RANCH

YES! Please send me the **Home on the Ranch Collection** in Larger Print. This collection begins with 3 FREE books and 2 FREE gifts in the first shipment. Along with my 3 free books, I'll also get the next 4 books from the Home on the Ranch Collection, in LARGER PRINT, which I may either return and owe nothing, or keep for the low price of $5.24 U.S./ $5.89 CDN each plus $2.99 for shipping and handling per shipment*. If I decide to continue, about once a month for 8 months I will get 6 or 7 more books, but will only need to pay for 4. That means 2 or 3 books in every shipment will be FREE! If I decide to keep the entire collection, I'll have paid for only 32 books because 19 books are FREE! I understand that accepting the 3 free books and gifts places me under no obligation to buy anything. I can always return a shipment and cancel at any time. My free books and gifts are mine to keep no matter what I decide.

268 HCN 3760 468 HCN 3760

Name	(PLEASE PRINT)
Address	Apt. #
City	State/Prov.	Zip/Postal Code

Signature (if under 18, a parent or guardian must sign)

Mail to the **Reader Service:**

IN U.S.A.: P.O. Box 1867, Buffalo, NY. 14240-1867
IN CANADA: P.O. Box 609, Fort Erie, Ontario L2A 5X3

* Terms and prices subject to change without notice. Prices do not include applicable taxes. Sales tax applicable in NY. Canadian residents will be charged applicable taxes. This offer is limited to one order per household. All orders subject to approval. Credit or debit balances in a customer's account(s) may be offset by any other outstanding balance owed by or to the customer. Please allow 3 to 4 weeks for delivery. Offer available while quantities last. Offer not available to Quebec residents.

HRCBPA18

READERSERVICE.COM

Manage your account online!

- Review your order history
- Manage your payments
- Update your address

We've designed the Reader Service website just for you.

Enjoy all the features!

- Discover new series available to you, and read excerpts from any series.
- Respond to mailings and special monthly offers.
- Browse the Bonus Bucks catalog and online-only exculsives.
- Share your feedback.

Visit us at:
ReaderService.com